FOREVER'S PROMISE

What Reviewers Say About Missouri Vaun's Work

Slow Burn

"This is the first book by Missouri Vaun that I've ever read and I wasn't sure how that was going to go. I'm pleased to say that I was not disappointed at all. In fact, I was hooked right at the first chapter and still had my undivided attention throughout the rest."
—*Lesbian Review*

"This book is like a breath of fresh air after a hard day. In fact, this is the kind of book I would grab to read after a bad day, or after reading something very intense. …This is a charming and tender romance with great characters, a wonderful setting, moments of excitement and lots of love. I really enjoyed this book, and I think you will too."—*Rainbow Reflections*

The Mandolin Lunch

"Two timid school teachers find love in this cozy lesbian contemporary from Vaun. The result is touching…"—*Publishers Weekly*

The Sea Within

"This is an amazing book. *The Sea Within* by Missouri Vaun is an exciting dystopian adventure and romance that will have you reading on the edge of your seat."—*Rainbow Reflections*

Chasing Sunset

"A road trip romance with good characters that had some nice chemistry."—Kat Adams, Bookseller (QBD Books, Australia)

"*Chasing Sunset* is a fun and enjoyable ride off into the sunset. Colorful characters, laughs and a sweet romance blend together to make a tasty read."—*Aspen Tree Book Reviews*

"This is a lovely summer romance. It has all the elements that you want in this type of novel: beautiful characters, great chemistry, lovely settings, and best of all, a nostalgic road trip across the country."—*Rainbow Reflections*

"I really liked this one! I found both Finn and Iris to be well fleshed out characters. Both women are trying to figure out their next steps, and that makes them both insecure about where their relationship is going. They have some major communication issues, but I found that, too, realistic. This was a low key read but very enjoyable. Recommended!"—Rebekah Miller, Librarian (University of Pittsburgh)

"The love story was tender and emotional and the sex was steamy and told so much about how intense their relationship was. I really enjoyed this story. Missouri Vaun has become one of my favourite authors and I'm never disappointed."—*Kitty Kat's Book Review Blog*

Spencer's Cove

"Just when I thought I knew where this story was going and who everyone was, Missouri Vaun took me on a ride that totally exceeded my expectations. …It was a magical tale and I absolutely adored it. Highly recommended."—*Kitty Kat's Book Reviews*

"The book is great fun. The chemistry between Abby and Foster is practically tangible. …Anyone who has seen and enjoyed the series *Charmed*, is going to be completely charmed by this rollicking romance."—*reviewer@large*

"Missouri Vaun has this way of taking me into the world she has created and does not let me out until I've finished the book." —*Les Rêveur*

"I was 100% all in after the first couple of pages and I wanted to call in sick, so I could stay home from work to immerse myself in this story. I've always enjoyed Missouri Vaun's books and I'm impressed with how she moves between genres with such ease. As paranormal stories go, this one left me thinking, 'Hmm, I wish I was part of that world,' and I've never read a book featuring vampires or weres that left me with that feeling. To sum it up, witches rock and Vaun made me a believer."—*Lesbian Review*

Take My Hand

"The chemistry between River and Clay is off the charts and their sex scenes were just plain hot!"—*Les Rêveur*

"The small town charms of *Take My Hand* evoke the heady perfume of pine needles and undergrowth, birdsong, and summer cocktails with friends."—*Omnivore Bibliosaur*

"I have a weakness for butch/femme couples so the Clay/River pairing worked for me, even if their names made me laugh. I like the way Missouri Vaun writes and felt like I got to know the folks in Pine Cone in just a few short scenes. The southern charm is front and center in *Take My Hand* and as River Hemsworth discovers, the locals are warm and welcoming."—*Late Night Lesbian Reviews*

Love at Cooper's Creek

"Blown away…how have I not read a book by Missouri Vaun before. *What* a beautiful love story which, honestly, I wasn't ready to finish. Kate and Shaw's chemistry was instantaneous and as the reader I could feel it radiating off the page."—*Les Reveur*

"Love at Cooper's Creek is a gentle, warm hug of a book."—*Lesbian Review*

"As always another well written book from Missouri Vaun—sweet romance with very little angst, well developed and likeable lead characters and a little family drama to spice things up."
—Melina Bickard, Librarian, Waterloo Library (UK)

Crossing the Wide Forever

"Crossing the Wide Forever is a near-heroic love story set in an epic time, told with almost lyrical prose. Words on the page will carry the reader, along with the main characters, back into history and into adventure. It's a tale that's easy to read, with enchanting main characters, despicable villains, and supportive friendships, producing a fascinating account of passion and adventure."
—*Lambda Literary Review*

Birthright

"The author develops a world that has a medieval feeling, complete with monasteries and vassal farmers, while also being a place and time where a lesbian relationship is just as legitimate and open as a heterosexual one. This kept pleasantly surprising me throughout my reading of the book. The adventure part of the story was fun, including traveling across kingdoms, on "wind-ships" across deserts, and plenty of sword fighting. …This book is worth reading for its fantasy world alone. In our world, where those in the LGBTQ communities still often face derision, prejudice, and danger for living and loving openly, being immersed in a world where the Queen can openly love another woman is a refreshing break from reality."
—Amanda Chapman, Librarian, Davisville Free Library (RI)

"Birthright by Missouri Vaun is one of the smoothest reads I've had my hands on in a long time."—*Lesbian Review*

The Time Before Now

"[*The Time Before Now*] is just so good. Vaun's character work in this novel is flawless. She told a compelling story about a person so real you could just about reach out and touch her."—*Lesbian Review*

The Ground Beneath

"One of my favourite things about Missouri Vaun's writing is her ability to write the attraction between two women. Somehow she manages to get that twinkle in the stomach just right and she makes me feel as if I am falling in love with my wife all over again."
—*Lesbian Review*

All Things Rise

"The futuristic world that author Missouri Vaun has brought to life is as interesting as it is plausible. The sci-fi aspect, though, is not hard-core which makes for easy reading and understanding of the technology prevalent in the cloud cities. ...[T]he focus was really on the dynamics of the characters especially Cole, Ava and Audrey--whether they were interacting on the ground or above the clouds. From the first page to the last, the writing was just perfect."—*AoBibliosphere*

"This is a lovely little Sci-Fi romance, well worth a read for anyone looking for something different. I will be keeping an eye out for future works by Missouri Vaun."—*Lesbian Review*

"Simply put, this book is easy to love. Everything about it makes for a wonderful read and re-read. I was able to go on a journey with these characters, an emotional, internal journey where I was able to take a look at the fact that while society and technology can change vastly until almost nothing remains the same, there are some fundamentals that never change, like hope, the raw emotion of human nature, and the far reaching search for the person who is able to soothe the fire in our souls with the love in theirs."—*Roses and Whimsy*

Writing as Paige Braddock

Jane's World and the Case of the Mail Order Bride

"This is such a quirky, sweet novel with a cast of memorable characters. It has laugh out loud moments and will leave you feeling charmed."—*Lesbian Review*

Visit us at www.boldstrokesbooks.com

By the Author

All Things Rise

The Time Before Now

The Ground Beneath

Whiskey Sunrise

Valley of Fire

Death By Cocktail Straw

One More Reason To Leave Orlando

Smothered and Covered

Privacy Glass

Birthright

Crossing The Wide Forever

Love At Cooper's Creek

Take My Hand

Proxima Five

Spencer's Cove

Chasing Sunset

The Sea Within

The Mandolin Lunch

Slow Burn

The Lonely Hearts Rescue

Forever's Promise

Writing as Paige Braddock:

Jane's World: The Case of the Mail Order Bride

FOREVER'S PROMISE

by
Missouri Vaun

2023

FOREVER'S PROMISE

ISBN 13: 978-1-63679-221-7

THIS TRADE PAPERBACK ORIGINAL IS PUBLISHED BY
BOLD STROKES BOOKS, INC.
P.O. BOX 249
VALLEY FALLS, NY 12185

FIRST EDITION: JULY 2023

CREDITS
EDITOR: CINDY CRESAP
PRODUCTION DESIGN: SUSAN RAMUNDO
COVER DESIGN BY TAMMY SEIDICK

Acknowledgments

I love westerns. I grew up watching them with my father. I always wished that those vintage westerns featured more women in varied roles. Women were as much a part of the frontier experience as men, but many of their stories are lost.

While researching this story I relied on first person journals of women who left comfortable homes to travel West with their families. There were also women who dressed as men to improve their chances for opportunity, among other reasons. This story is a work of fiction, but it draws details from the real experiences of women who settled in Kansas in the 1850s.

I'd like to thank my beta readers, especially Jenny Harmon, who redirected an early draft of this story and got it back on track. Thank you to D. Jackson Leigh also. I never want to write about horses without your input, Deb. Special thanks to my editor, Cindy. And to Sandy, Rad, and Ruth for all the continued support. I'm always grateful to be a part of the BSB family.

Lastly, thank you to my wife, Evelyn, for joining me on this adventure.

Dedication

To the brave women who inspired this story.

CHAPTER ONE

Wesley Holden and her brother, Clyde, had built this homestead in Kansas together, from nothing. Every time Wes walked the fields, her chest filled with pride at what they'd accomplished so far. Yes, it had been grueling at times, but ultimately, they would gain from whatever effort they put in—and that was rewarding on every level.

Back in Tennessee, there'd been pressure from her aunt and uncle to marry. Most young women her age were already with child. But matrimony felt like one more cage she needed to escape. When she abandoned her dresses for trousers, she'd done just that.

In the beginning, she'd felt self-conscious and worried she'd be found out, but as time went on she became more relaxed. She was tall and a bit lanky, with no obvious curve to her hips. And her chest was easy to disguise. No one gave her a second glance. Especially if she let Clyde do most of the talking. He'd gotten on board with the idea quickly. Traveling with a brother was a lot less complicated than traveling with a sister. Plus, it was a lot easier to do the work required to homestead in britches. Wes reasoned that her manner of dress was practical and pragmatic. It just felt right.

The frontier was open to anyone brave enough to make the trip. When Clyde suggested they stake a claim in Kansas, Wes jumped at the chance to go along. The unknown edge of the frontier was frightening but at the same time offered the freedom she feared she'd never find in Tennessee amongst her people. She used the phrase *her people*, but at the same time considered herself separate from them. Kin, but not kindred.

In pretty much every settled part of the world, home was regarded as the proper place for women. Women were expected to serve diligently as wives and mothers and housekeepers. None of those things suited Wes. She desired something, or someplace, uncommon or unique. She wanted something more for her life. Not that domestic life wasn't important, it just didn't agree with her. Most girls took to it so easily. She'd watched her cousins shift to marriage and domestic life seamlessly. The pressure to follow suit was building, and she'd wanted desperately to escape the inevitable.

The first winter had been hard. Made even harder by the fact that the house was not fully constructed. They had to fell timber and notch the logs, and Wes had to be taught things about carpentry as they went. But she was eager to learn and threw her whole heart into the enterprise.

The next year, they ran the sod cutter over the ground, harrowed it, then seeded it with corn. Corn did well in Kansas. They smoked meat, dried fruit, and basically ate corn in every way imaginable—bread, grits, mush, pudding, and even pancakes. There was almost a comforting monotony to it all. There was contentment in having control over your own life. Even down to what food you ate each day and how. Clyde and Wes shared kitchen duty equally. This farm, despite the hard labor, had become almost paradise for her.

Wes straightened from her work on the north end of the field as Clyde approached.

"I think I'm done for the day." He tipped the brim of his hat up, but his eyes were in shadow.

"I've got a bit more to do." Wes rotated her back to the sun so that she could see him better. "You okay?" It wasn't like Clyde to leave the field this early. Some days he'd work until it was so dark you couldn't see your hand in front of your face. That was the nature of building something from nothing. You had to give it everything you had.

"Just thought I might go round us up some grub. Something besides corn." He grinned and turned his head to check the angle of the sun. "I can get some hunting in before dark." He removed his hat and wiped his brow with his shirtsleeve.

"You want me to come along?"

"Why, so you can scare off the wildlife?" He always made the same joke, even though it was usually Clyde who scared off the game with his whistling, which he frequently did without being aware of it.

"Suit yourself, but you know I'm a better shot."

"Ha!" He laughed. "We'll see about that, baby sister."

Wes smiled and waved him off.

"Go on then. I'll just be here finishing your work for you."

He smiled broadly and adjusted his hat.

She watched him amble back toward the barn to saddle his horse.

CHAPTER TWO

Dust swirled in small puffs, stirred by the hem of her long skirt as Charlotte Rose crossed the street to the boarding house. This early in the day, St. Louis had a special sort of urban energy. In the previous decades, the city on the river had transitioned from a center for trappers and fur traders to a hub of commerce. Factories and warehouses populated the northern boundary of the city by 1850. Spreading out from the riverfront were houses, storefronts, brass and iron foundries, and a mill.

It wasn't easy to be a single woman in the city even under the best circumstances. Even in a city with as much industry and opportunity as St. Louis. Some women perished from want, others were tempted into crime because of poverty. A woman only received half price for the work she did but was required to pay full price for everything she needed. This was a reality Charlotte was confronted with every day.

The hinges of the door to the boarding house squeaked as she pushed through it and crossed the threshold. A rug that had seen better days ran the length of the entryway. It was faded from boarders and passersby. To the left was a parlor with a few upholstered chairs, to the right a dining room with a long table. Charlotte began to regret that she'd come. Her actions might seem desperate, but she hadn't heard from Nathaniel in days. She glanced quickly to survey the room. The seating area inside the parlor was empty except for one man reading the paper and smoking. He glanced over at Charlotte and then returned to the news of the day. The smoke from his cigar hung like a blue haze around him. The sun filtering through the smoke gave the entire scene an otherworldly aura.

"Can I help you, miss?" A middle-aged woman came from the dining room off to the right. The kitchen door swung closed behind her with a whoosh as she walked toward the entry. Charlotte jumped at the sound of her curt question.

"Um, hello." Charlotte swept her bonnet off and let it hang from a ribbon around her neck. "I'm asking after Nathaniel Finch. Is he here?"

The woman pursed her lips, an expression of recognition on her face.

"No, he's no longer here." She stood closer to Charlotte and lowered her voice even though the man in the parlor seemed to be paying them no mind. "I'm fairly certain he won't be back. And good riddance." The woman softened her expression and regarded Charlotte with a look that she interpreted as somewhere between judgment and pity.

"Are you quite sure?"

"I can see you're troubled." The woman tried to be kind. "Trust me. It's better that he left. A pretty girl like you—a lady—doesn't need the likes of Nathaniel Finch." She touched Charlotte's arm for emphasis.

Charlotte nodded but was afraid to speak because the lump in her throat would choke the words. She'd made the trip from the levees, past the livery, to this boarding house hoping to solve the mystery of Nathaniel's silence. He could have been injured, or ill, but it seemed he'd simply disappeared.

She had to come to terms with the reality that Nathaniel was gone and she'd been left without a word or a promise. He'd taken advantage of her affection and callously tossed her aside. The tears that hovered at the edge of her lashes were as much rooted in anger as hurt. She would not allow herself to cry over a man who obviously cared so little for her.

Charlotte swayed on her feet. She brought her handkerchief quickly from her small handbag and held it to her lips. She wasn't sure if it was lack of breakfast or the harsh reality of her situation that caused the sudden nausea. She squeezed her eyes shut and focused on breathing.

"Oh, wait a minute. He did leave a letter." The woman walked to a wardrobe in the entry and returned with an envelope in her hand. "Are you Charlotte?"

She nodded and took the letter.

"Would you like to sit for a little while with me in the kitchen? You don't seem well."

Charlotte shook her head.

"Thank you, but I should go."

"Are you sure you're alright?" The woman wasn't convinced.

"I'm fine, thank you." She said the words, with no idea of whether they were true or not. Would she be fine? She wasn't at all confident of that fact. Charlotte turned to leave before her emotions got away from her.

Charlotte hesitated once she was on the porch. Her stomach sank and she imagined the world dropping away to nothing. She could simply step off into oblivion. If only that were possible. She swallowed and slowly descended the stairs to the dusty road.

It wasn't that Nathaniel had forced her to do something she didn't want to, not exactly, but he'd been so insistent. And she was fond of him, but perhaps she'd been most drawn to his sense of adventure. She'd found herself swept along with his grand plans to travel west and believed him when he said he'd take care of her. Nothing he'd said was true, except the part about his desire to find his fortune out west. Had he ever intended to take her with him? That seemed unlikely now.

She'd always made allowances for human frailty, so initially she gave him the benefit of the doubt. But after days with no word and now hearing from the innkeeper that he wouldn't be back, doubt turned to certainty. She'd been too naive and trusting, and Nathaniel had been a very convincing liar.

She opened the envelope. Inside was a note that said only, *I'm sorry*, and a stagecoach ticket. The question Charlotte now faced was, what to do? She couldn't stay here with everyone knowing she'd been deserted. Could she? Why did he leave her the ticket? He must have considered taking her with him, but then abandoned the idea just as he'd abandoned her.

She started to cross the street half in a daze.

"Careful, miss!" A man put his arm in front of her to block her path.

She'd been so distracted that she'd almost stepped out in front of an approaching team of horses. The man paused for a moment and regarded her with a stern expression before continuing up the street. Charlotte chided herself for not paying attention. It was still early in the day, but the streets had come to life with the business of the day. She should be more careful.

Charlotte checked both ways this time before crossing the street. She had to start work soon and if she didn't hurry, she'd be late.

CHAPTER THREE

Wes stood in the cabin doorway and debated what she should do. Dark was coming and Clyde should've been back home hours ago. If she struck out now, tracks would be impossible to follow once nighttime caught up with her. And chances were just as good that he'd ride back and they'd pass each other in the darkness without knowing. It was probably best to sit tight and wait for daybreak, even though that was the last thing she wanted to do.

There was no light tonight, no moon to make shadows. Wes heard an eerie owl call in the distance, but all she could see of the prairie that surrounded the dwelling was the small patch of soft, golden candlelight cast by the open door. Wes turned slowly and went back inside. She hung her hat on a peg by the door, carried the candle to her bedroom, and undressed for sleep. First, she took off her boots and set them side by side on the rough floorboards at the end of the narrow bed, then her trousers, and then her shirt. The Henley undershirt came next, and the last task was to remove the thin strips of cloth that hid her breasts. Wes slowly unwound the material and rubbed her palms across her chest. Having been liberated from her disguise, she tugged on a nightshirt and stretched out on the straw mattress. Unfortunately, sleep eluded her even though she'd spent a full day working in the field. Her arms and back were fatigued, but her mind wouldn't rest.

Every sound, every creak of the log walls settling or the wind, made her think Clyde was home. The tiny cabin on the exposed prairie at night was what Wes imagined a ship felt like on the dark open sea. No other flickers of light or civilization within view. The vast grasslands at night were equal parts lonely and eerily magical. Wes took a deep breath and rolled onto her side to face away from the open window to wait for morning. She tried her best not to worry, but that was a nearly impossible task.

In the end, she figured she'd only dozed off the last hour before sunrise.

Wes set coffee to boil over the fire while she dressed in the cool morning air of early spring. It would be chilly to start with, but when the sun revealed itself the temp would warm. She stood at the cabin window swigging the coffee and chewing a strip of venison before she reached for her hat and strode to the barn to saddle her horse. Dusty's breath puffed white in the chilled air as Wes tightened the flank cinch. She gripped the saddle horn with her left hand as she slid her boot in the stirrup and swung up into the saddle with one strong motion.

"Easy, boy." Wes leaned forward and rubbed Dusty's neck to settle him. Maybe he'd picked up on her unease and worry about her brother.

It wasn't like him to stay out for so long. Normally, if Clyde went hunting in the afternoon he'd return before dark or shortly thereafter, whether he got anything or not. The fact that he hadn't turned up had Wes's insides in a knot of concern.

They left the barn and she angled Dusty northwest, following hoofprints left by Clyde's horse, Ned. Spring rains had given way to brighter weather the past few days. Buds on the cottonwood trees were bursting open all along the river. Blue, yellow, and violet wildflowers painted the eastern Kansas grasslands with color. The vegetable garden had begun to show. Tender sprigs of green peeked through the dark soil of the plowed fields.

With the cabin nothing more than a dark square on the southern horizon, Wes turned west, following Clyde's path through the trees and across the creek. Eventually, the grove thinned and the landscape transitioned again to prairie. The tall grass was an undulating sea of golden brown against the crisp blue sky.

The day had warmed a bit, and she unbuttoned her jacket but didn't take it off.

Wes hadn't seen any tracks since leaving the tree line. But every now and then the grass was beat down in such a way that she could tell a horse had passed. The longer her search took, the more uneasy she became about what she'd find.

Anything could have happened to Clyde in this remote outpost on the Kansas frontier. His rifle could have misfired or his horse could've been spooked by a snake. It was even possible to cross paths with a native hunting party and find yourself rife with arrows. Wes was on high alert, continually stopping to listen and repeatedly scanning the horizon.

She kept heading in a westerly direction for another hour or so until she saw the dark shape of something in the distance. She slowed and cautiously approached. They owned one rifle between them, and Clyde had taken it with him to hunt. The only weapon Wes carried was a knife in a sheath on her belt. A knife required a close fight, and she was still too far away for it to be useful.

As she drew near, she could see that the brown shape she'd seen was Clyde's horse, Ned. He stopped grazing and raised his head as she and Dusty approached. His reins drooped to the ground. One boot hung askew in the stirrup, but otherwise, there was no sign of Clyde.

Wes dismounted and checked Ned over. The rifle was still strapped to the saddle. There were no visible injuries. She gathered Ned's and Dusty's reins into one hand and scanned the area.

"Clyde!" She called his name and waited for a response.

The grass was so tall that if Clyde was injured and on the ground she'd never be able to see him. She dropped the reins and started walking in a slowly expanding circle, working her way from where she'd found Ned outward.

As it turned out, Ned hadn't strayed too far. She found Clyde lying on his back. He was looking up at the sky with a neutral expression on his face, as if he were watching clouds pass overhead. It was the stillness of his gaze that unsettled her.

"Clyde?" She knelt beside him and touched his hand. His skin was cold. She leaned close to his face, placing her cheek right over his nose and mouth. He wasn't breathing. She gently closed his eyes with her fingertips and sank back on her heels.

A chill ran up her arms.

Her chest began to rise and fall in sharp, deep breaths. Wes feared she might pass out. She lurched to her feet, staggered several yards away and threw up. She wiped her mouth with her sleeve and walked away from Clyde into the empty grassland. Wes crossed her arms almost as if she were hugging herself and paced back and forth. She stopped once and bent over, with her hands braced on her knees. After a little while, her stomach settled and she stood up.

Eventually, her stunned brain was able to take in more details from the scene.

Several yards away a rock was smeared with blood. The grass from that stone to where Clyde rested had been broken and pressed down. He'd obviously fallen from the saddle and hit his head. Given one boot was still with Ned, Clyde had probably been dragged from where he fell.

Wes buried her face in the crook of her arm as if hiding the scene from view would make it less real.

There was no future Wes imagined for herself that Clyde wasn't in.

They had come to the Kansas territory to build a life for themselves. A life of their own design by their own hands.

Maybe this was even more true for Wes, although she would not presume to know the inner workings of her brother's mind. Clyde was quiet and kept his own counsel. But he was her only family. They depended on each other possibly more than most siblings, who at their age might have gone separate ways to start a family.

Their parents had passed when she and Clyde were children. Relatives had taken them in, but amongst her cousins, Wes felt apart—other. It was hard to put a name to the feeling. Clyde was the only person in the world she trusted completely. He was the only person who knew her. He *was* her family. And now he was gone.

Wes knelt down, removed her hat, and rested her cheek on Clyde's chest. She waited, hoping against hope that she'd hear a faint heartbeat. But there was no movement, no sudden restart of his heart. He was no longer with her. He was utterly still and lifeless. It was strange to see the shape of his body next to her but feel his absence so strongly. Whatever happened to someone when they died, they for sure left their physical self behind. She knew without a doubt that Clyde was no longer with her.

Wes straightened from her kneeling position and stood up. She surveyed the open landscape. The sky was too big to believe sometimes, and the air carried the scent of nearby wild roses. The place where Clyde lay was surrounded by low rolling hills and an unobstructed view of the horizon. Fleecy clouds driven by a gentle wind passed overhead. She took a deep breath and closed her eyes. When the wind stirred her hair, she opened them again.

There was no use waiting any longer. She led the horses to where Clyde lay and using a rope tied to the horn of her saddle, walked Dusty in the opposite direction to hoist his body up onto Ned's back. She felt oddly detached from herself. She was going through the motions of what had to be done, but every movement, every step was as if she was watching herself do things from a distance. A lump had settled in her throat, but the tears hadn't come.

Wes climbed into the saddle and turned the horses toward home.

CHAPTER FOUR

The kitchen was bustling when Charlotte stepped through the back door of the hotel. She hung her bonnet and bag on a peg in the hallway and then reached for a fresh apron from the folded stack just inside the entrance to the maid's supply room. Clinking glassware and the hum of voices joined the buzzing of thoughts inside her head. This place, the work, felt familiar and safe. This was a place she knew. For the rest of the day, she could lose herself in chores.

Charlotte allowed her eyes to lose focus as she stared out a small window over the linen cupboard and absently wrapped the apron strings around her waist, cinching them into a tight knot.

"Are you alright?" Alice was suddenly right beside her. Alice was a wisp of a girl, barely eighteen, with a single blond braid down her back and freckles across her nose. "You seem upset."

Alice and Charlotte shared a rented room in a boarding house for young women not too far from the hotel. It was hard to keep secrets in a small space, so of course, Alice knew about Nathaniel. Or at least part of the story. There was no way Charlotte could tell Alice everything; she was too embarrassed.

"I'm fine. Just feeling a little tired is all." Charlotte tried her best to smile. It had been a couple of days since receiving the letter Nathaniel had left for her, and she still hadn't quite figured out what to do. She pulled the envelope from her bag and slipped it into the front pocket of her apron.

"Oh, you have a letter. Are you going to open it?" Alice's question was full of friendly curiosity and excitement.

"Later."

"How can you stand to wait?"

There was no privacy in the kitchen area. She already knew the letter wasn't good news, it wasn't even really a letter, but Charlotte kept rereading the two-word apology hoping to find some truth behind the words. The note, after all, was the last thread of connection to Nathaniel.

"Chat on your own time, ladies." Mrs. Arden appeared in the doorway. Her full frame almost filling the open door from side to side.

"Yes, ma'am." Charlotte nodded.

Charlotte and Alice gathered cleaning supplies and clean linens and climbed the stairs to the second floor. At the top of the stairs, they split up to work in different rooms.

She thought back to that day when she'd first met Nathaniel in the hotel dining room. Charlotte had been tempted by Nathaniel. He'd made many empty promises to her. She saw that clearly now. She'd been so utterly innocent to the dangers of a man like Nathaniel. Could she ever truly recover from such a betrayal?

Her days had been spent in the drudgery of existing. Charlotte worked long hours for food and board and even still was barely scraping by. Society allowed men certain freedoms that women dared not sample. The inequity of life sometimes made Charlotte angry, and there seemed to be nowhere to direct those feelings.

It seemed that Alice never had such dark thoughts. Charlotte sometimes envied Alice's simple acceptance of life. Charlotte couldn't help wanting more, although she wasn't exactly sure what *more* meant.

Most of the rooms on the second floor were vacant by midday. She walked to the room at the end of the hallway in hopes of privacy with her thoughts.

Charlotte stripped the sheets from the bed as she waited for the right moment to examine the note and the ticket again. She sat at the edge of the mattress. Her heart pounded in her chest.

Charlotte held the envelope to her face and breathed it in. Sometime between finding Nathaniel gone and showing up for work, she'd pretty much decided that she would leave St. Louis as soon as possible. She would chart her own path. She was tired of waiting on some man to liberate her. She would embark on her own western adventure. Thoughts swirled in her head. There was trepidation, for sure, but also hope for a better life. And a family of her own. That would be worth the risk, regardless of how far she had to travel to attain it.

CHAPTER FIVE

A clap of thunder startled Wes, and she jolted awake, unsure of her surroundings for a moment. She'd fallen asleep in her clothes, exhausted from digging Clyde's grave.

Lightning flashed, dowsing the room with brightness for an instant. Several seconds later, the sound of thunder followed, a deep rumbling that seemed to travel across the earth to the soles of her feet. She shivered and hugged herself.

The storm-cooled air had seeped in through the open window, lowering the temperature of the room. Wes closed the window, which had no glass, only shutters.

The front door banged loudly. She thought she'd put the bar in place to secure it, but obviously she'd forgotten. She wasn't quite herself since finding Clyde's body.

Wes got to her feet and shuffled across the room. She stood in the open doorway facing the wind for a moment before she stepped outside. Several heavy drops of rain pelted the ground around her. One hit her in the forehead. Then more drops, large and slanted at an angle by a tailwind. She couldn't see the rain, but she could hear it and feel it. The moon and stars were gone. All that remained was a churning darkness overhead that matched her mood.

The rain was falling in sheets now. Her soaked shirt suctioned itself to her body. Wes swept her fingers through her hair, brushing her bangs up away from her forehead. She braced her feet and leaned into the storm defiantly.

And then from somewhere deep inside, something began to build. She could feel the force of it pulse at her temples. She squeezed her eyes shut and raged into the wind, her shout swallowed by the gale. A gust caused her to stumble backward before she dropped to her knees in the mud. She was scared and angry and she wasn't even sure why or at whom to direct her rage.

If God were to speak wouldn't it sound like thunder? Was the wind God's breath? Sensing the Almighty's nearness, Wes began to silently pray. After everything they'd been through, couldn't God come to her aid? She needed her brother more now than ever and he was gone. Did God not even care?

Wes clenched her fists and pounded the damp earth. Maybe God had no time for those who lost touch. She hadn't prayed in a long, long time. Perhaps God no longer listened.

Rain soaked her skin, cooling her heated cheeks.

After a little while, her rage turned to tears.

Her tears mingled with the rain until she began to shiver from the cold. Her drenched clothing was heavy, making it hard for her to regain her footing as the storm swirled around her. Wes probably should have been frightened, but she wasn't.

She stumbled through the darkness into the cabin and slipped the wooden board into the grooves to hold the door in place. She stood next to the hearth and began to peel her sopping shirt away. She draped it over a nearby chair and then bent to stir the coals. She added a little wood to warm the room and dry her things.

She sat for a long while and stared at the fire, mesmerized by the dancing flames. Wes had allowed herself this small space to fall apart, but she had to pull herself together. The farm wouldn't take care of itself, and now all of it fell to her shoulders. She'd wanted independence more than anything else. Hell, she'd dressed as a man and traveled a thousand miles just to find a place where she could be herself.

She'd do whatever it took to keep the claim, but could she really do it alone?

Wes redirected her thoughts. She couldn't think about the whole enterprise all at once. She just needed to focus on one small task at a time, and then one task would lead to the next. She knew how to run a farm. She knew how to hunt. Wes had all the skills she'd need. The key was not to fall behind. If things got away from her she'd never catch up.

Wes knew that if the situation was reversed Clyde would want her to carry on. And to honor his memory, she'd do exactly that.

She took the rest of her wet clothing off and hung it over a chair by the fire to dry. She tugged on a nightshirt and settled under the covers. The storm had subsided and all that remained was the haunting sound of the wind in the cottonwoods along the creek.

The thought of Clyde under the wet, cold earth kept her from sleeping. She tried to picture other things. She closed her eyes and visualized memories of their childhood in the Tennessee hills where everything was green and summers were long and nights were warm. She thought of fireflies and the scent of honeysuckle and the dew on the lush grass.

She rolled onto her side. She could see the glow of the fire from the other room. Shadows danced along the wall making her feel a bit less lonely. But the truth was, she was alone. And she felt it in the deepest part of her being.

CHAPTER SIX

The day of Charlotte's departure had finally arrived. The morning dawned brightly, and she stood on the landing of the stage office, ticket in hand, awaiting her destiny. From where she stood, Charlotte could see the facade of the hotel where she'd spent so many working hours. The morning sun bounced off the windows, which caused her to shield her eyes.

She clinched her fingers around the ticket for fear it would slip her grasp before the coach arrived. This was simultaneously the most exciting and most terrifying thing she'd ever done.

Charlotte had no family left to miss, no one to talk her out of this bold, potentially reckless adventure, except Alice. She'd truly been on her own since she was fourteen. Her mother had slipped away late one night after a long illness leaving Charlotte utterly alone. Charlotte had learned from her mother how much the heart can bear and still continue to beat. A lesson she would carry with her throughout her life.

At nineteen, it was beyond time for Charlotte to try for something new, something bigger than working as a maid six days a week. She'd done nothing but sweep up and clean behind others' adventures. It was long past time for her to have an adventure of her own. She was sure there were opportunities in the West that she could only dream of here. There was nothing left for her here.

She'd left Alice early. They'd shared a tearful good-bye just after dawn, with a promise to write. Alice had work to attend. There would be no one to stand with her and wave good-bye as the stage pulled away from the landing. But maybe that was just as well. Another tearful good-bye would only serve to shake her resolve.

Travel by stagecoach was particularly convenient for women alone or with children. But this morning no one else awaited departure.

Stage travelers were advised to wear old clothing for the journey. It was best to wear something you did not mind getting dusty, muddy, or wrinkled. Charlotte had a limited wardrobe, but she'd chosen a calico dress for the trip, assuming it would show less wear from travel. She had a shawl for the chill of early morning. Which sometimes could be felt even in the summer.

Men were advised to wear clothes suited for work. They might have to help put on a wheel or pull the coach out of a mudhole.

Charlotte turned her attention toward the street. She heard the stage before she saw it. The coach arrived amidst the thundering hooves of four horses and a cloud of dust in front of the stage office. Charlotte took a few steps back as the driver tugged the reins to settle the animals. The horses snorted loudly and stomped their feet as if anxious to depart, which only served to keep dust particles lingering in the air. Charlotte realized she might be a frightful sight from travel when she reached her destination. It would be hard to make a good impression on anyone after several days in an open coach.

"Can I get your bag, miss?" A man had joined her on the landing from the driver's seat at the front of the coach. Like everything else, his clothes and boots were covered with a fine brown powder. His face was weathered but friendly.

"Yes, thank you." She held her bags out to him.

He placed the carpeted satchels on top of the coach and then held the door and offered his hand for her to climb in. The interior of the coach was rather dark. The shades had been drawn to no doubt keep the dust from invading the compartment. Two wide seats inside the coach faced each other. Charlotte took a seat and realized quickly that her only company was a roll of freshly tanned leather as large as a sleeping man placed diagonally across the seats. The bottom of the coach was rounded and hung on springs that caused it to rock back and forth in a swaying motion as other goods for transport were mounted on top.

Charlotte was somewhat relieved to have this big moment of departure for herself. She was about to embark on an epic journey. She was about to submit her life and fortunes to not only the man who held the reins of the coach, but to the unknown.

The stage lurched forward, and she felt the stiff seat at her back. Charlotte gripped the small cloth bag in her lap, willed her stomach to settle, and closed her eyes. She let out a long, slow breath. As the stage gained speed, Charlotte lifted the window covering closest to her and watched as the city that had become so familiar slipped past.

CHAPTER SEVEN

Wes looked back once before she left the cabin to begin the day's routine work. There was so much to do that she wasn't sure what to do first. Normally, she was clearheaded, but this morning what had happened to Clyde had her insides all churned up and it was making her head foggy with distraction.

She headed to the barn. She'd take care of the horses first. She'd let them out and then walk the field and see what needed tending. The day was overcast, but the air didn't smell like rain. More rain would be welcomed. So far, this spring had been a bit too dry for her liking.

Wes took a few minutes to add some fresh hay for the horses before she headed out to the field. She glanced back at the house from the barn half expecting to see Clyde appear in the doorway. It had been nearly a month since she'd buried him and still her mind couldn't quite grasp the finality of his passing. But the farm was beginning to show his absence. Wes was just one person and now she had to do the work of two. She was barely keeping up.

Ned, Clyde's horse, nuzzled against Wes's arm as she opened the gate in the barn for him. She wondered if he could sense her distress. Animals sometimes seemed to know things. She rubbed his neck as he walked past. Dusty hung back, as if he was waiting for something. He was smaller than Ned, but what Dusty lacked in height, he made up for in heart.

"What's wrong, boy?" Wes patted Dusty and checked the hay on the floor for anything odd. A snake could have gotten in the pen, or some other critter that might have made Dusty skittish. She didn't see anything. Possibly Dusty sensed a storm. Whatever was bothering him seemed to abate after a brief rubdown. He sauntered out toward the fenced, grassy area beside the barn and lowered his head to eat not too far from Ned.

Within an hour, the sun was breaking through the clouds and the air had warmed. It was a perfect spring day. Wes took a break from field work to splash some water on her face from the stream and take a few sips. She cupped her hand and with quick motions brought cool relief to her lips. She swallowed quickly, slurping the water from her hand before it had time to escape between her fingers. Wes dried her hand on the front of her shirt because it was cleaner than her trousers. She decided she'd do a bit more work and then try to choke down some lunch. Grief and loneliness had ruined her appetite and her sleep.

Before leaving the stream, she took her handkerchief off, soaked it in the cool water, and then tied it back around her neck. As she strode toward the freshly cleaned row of corn sprouts, she saw a man on horseback approaching.

It was Ben Caufield. He and his wife, Maddie, had a farm just south of their claim. The Caufield's had two children, Joseph and Rachel. Ben and Maddie had been good neighbors to them when they first arrived. They'd brought food and Ben and Joseph had even helped with the cabin roof. Joseph was only seven, but he helped fetch things and was surprisingly good with a hammer for a youngster. Neighbors were few and far between, so they tried to check in on each other whenever they were passing by, which wasn't that often.

"Hello there." Ben waved as he got nearer.

"Hey." Wes walked to the edge of the plowed field and leaned on the long handle of the hoe. She mostly let Clyde do the talking when men were around for fear of giving herself away. But Clyde wasn't here. She needed to get used to that.

"How's it looking?" Ben surveyed the field from the saddle of his horse. He was about thirty, with a thick light brown beard and unruly short blond hair. Ben was a stout fellow, twice as wide as Wes, but not as tall. His neck and cheeks bore a perpetual sunburn from long hours of farming. Laugh lines were etched all around his blue eyes. He had a likeable manner.

"The corn seems to be coming along." She followed his gaze. "I think."

"We could use some more rain." He tipped the brim of his hat up and looked at the sky.

"Yeah, we could." Wes focused on keeping her voice even and her phrases short.

"Clyde's not workin' today?" There was no judgment in Ben's question, just curiosity.

"No, um, he um…he had an accident a few weeks back."

"How bad?" Ben refocused on Wes. There was genuine concern in his voice.

"He…he didn't make it." Wes shifted her weight from one foot to the other, still leaning on the hoe handle. She hadn't seen anyone since the day she'd buried Clyde, and she wasn't sure she could even talk about what happened without getting choked up. She looked away for fear she'd reveal too much.

"I can't believe it." Ben swung down from his horse but still kept a respectable distance from Wes.

"Me either." Wes wasn't sure how much to say. They were neighbors, but it wasn't as if she was close to Ben. He'd always talked more to Clyde.

"You need anything?"

Wes shook her head and stared at the ground.

"I'm—" Her voice cracked, choking her words. She cleared her throat. "I'm okay, thank you."

There was an awkward moment of silence. Wes didn't blame Ben for not knowing what to say. She didn't know what to say either and she'd had more time to come to terms with the reality of Clyde's death than he had.

Ben climbed back into the saddle. He could probably sense her inability to talk about it. Thankfully, he didn't push for more.

"Maddie and I will check in with you in a few days, okay?" Ben adjusted his hat so the brim shadowed his eyes again.

Wes nodded.

It was a relief simply to share the burden with someone. For another person to know that things were not okay. For all her striving at freedom and autonomy, she had still relied on her brother quite a bit. Without him, she felt a little lost. She stood for a while watching Ben ride into the distance.

❖

By the time Wes started back to the house it was past midday and the clouds had broken up into smaller puffy versions of themselves. A cloud passed in front of the sun for only a moment and then the sun broke through again. She'd worked up a good sweat by the time she reached the porch. She scraped clods of dirt from the sides of her boots so as not to track even more unnecessary debris from the field inside. The porch was more like a stoop. A short overhang and two half-hewn log steps. Sometimes Wes liked to sit on the logs in the doorway and watch the sun set. But mostly it wasn't the sort of stoop you could lounge on. There was enough room for Clyde and Wes to sit side by side, but that had rarely happened.

Building a farm from nothing was a full-time thing. Wes worked from sunup to sundown and found that she had very little time to sit and reflect. As far as she was concerned, representations of nature as a fond mother suckling her young were far from the truth. Those who had lived close to the wild frontier knew nature to be a tyrant, void of mercy from whom nothing would be won without hard work and great personal sacrifice. The reward to those who endured was the most outright independence that existed anywhere. Personal independence made all the labor of carving a life here worthwhile in Wes's opinion. Freedom to be exactly who she wanted to be had become her most valued possession. Even if she hadn't quite allowed it to sink in.

Sometimes, Wes felt that her life had been nothing but one long, hard war against elemental powers. Because of her parents' death when she was still a child, the first lesson life had taught Wes was self-reliance. But not complete self-reliance because she had Clyde. He'd taught her so many things since leaving Tennessee for the unknown. She wasn't sure she could have done any of this without him.

She allowed herself to feel a few moments of gratitude for her brother and for everything she'd learned from him. At least if she was going to be alone she'd much rather be alone here on her own terms than back in Tennessee.

The school of the prairie frontier was harsh and stern. But the sky was big and the land was open. A person could discover themselves here. Wes felt sure of it. She squinted at the sun's brightness before she stepped into the dim interior of the cabin.

CHAPTER EIGHT

Charlotte Rose shielded her eyes with her hand as the large bird circled again overhead, its dark wings silhouetted across the sun. The sky was cloudless and the sunbaked earth all around where she lay was as dry as her throat. She had no idea how long she'd been lying on the hard ground. There was a dull banging sound that for a minute she thought was inside her head, but then realized that the open door of the stagecoach was moving in the light breeze. Her temple throbbed and her shoulder ached. When she touched the side of her head lightly with her fingers, she felt something slick, and when she held her hand up again she could see that her fingertips were red with blood.

Charlotte tried to sit up, but her head was swimming. She rolled onto her side instead and then gradually raised up on one arm to a seated position. The stagecoach was only a few feet away. If she'd fallen underneath it she'd at least have been in the shade, but instead she felt the sting of a sunburn on her cheeks and forehead. The horses were gone. The two men who'd been on the stage with her, along with the driver, were lying on the ground, unmoving. Baggage had clearly been ransacked. Clothing and sundries were scattered all over. Some papers fluttered past her and into the endless prairie that surrounded where she sat.

Braced with one arm, using the spokes of the large wheel like a ladder, Charlotte managed to get to her feet. She took a few deep breaths and leaned into the shadow of the stagecoach to get her bearings. She checked each of the men for signs of life and found none. Blood soaked the ground around them and flies had gathered.

They'd been attacked, but by whom? Had the stage been carrying something of value? She had no idea. Everything she had in the world she'd carried from St. Louis in two carpet bags, and it was now scattered all over the rutted Santa Fe Trail. She slowly gathered her clothing and folded it haphazardly and shoved it back in the bags, dust and all. As she repacked her things, Charlotte took stock of her situation, which wasn't good. She wasn't exactly sure where she was. A half day's ride from Hollister, in the territory of Kansas, and as far as the eye could see nothing but prairie from where she stood to the horizon.

At the moment, thirst seemed more pressing than geography. Charlotte left her bag on the ground and searched the coach for water. It was a challenge to reach the driver's high bench seat, but she was rewarded by a partially filled canteen. The water was warm but soothed her parched throat. The first swig brought on a coughing fit, but then she finished off the rest. Only after drinking the last of it did the thought occur to her that maybe it would have been more prudent to save a little in case she was stranded for more than a few hours. Which, given her proximity to the back of beyond, seemed likely.

Charlotte stood in the tracks of the stagecoach and searched in every direction. She was afraid to linger. It made sense to assume that she'd only survived because the men who stopped them had believed she was dead. She shielded her eyes from the sun and scanned the horizon one more time. It seemed terrible to leave the others where they lay, but she didn't know what choice she had. She decided the best plan was to walk back in the direction they'd come. At least if she walked east she knew she'd eventually reach Hollister. Although, Charlotte had no idea how long that would take.

❖

After walking for quite some time, Charlotte came to a trail that cut away to the south from the main path. She stood at the crossroads and considered what to do. Perhaps this trail would lead to a farm, which would be closer than trying to make it all the way to Hollister on foot. The sun was low in the sky, and she didn't want to be out in the open after dark. Her shoulders and arms ached from carrying the two bags and she was very thirsty. She set the bags down and touched the side of her face. The bleeding had stopped, but she could feel dried blood on her cheek and temple. Her head still throbbed, but it was impossible to know if it hurt from the wound or from the sun or from thirst. In any event, the shock was beginning to wear off, and in its place, panic was creeping in.

The openness of the landscape was so vast that it was hard to have any sense of context. Charlotte had gotten so used to the hemmed-in existence of St. Louis that the stark prairie was a bit of a shock to her system. But there was something in the distance to the south. Something she hadn't noticed at first. A dark shape just slightly broke the sameness of the grassy landscape. Charlotte considered that what she was seeing might be her fatigued brain playing tricks on her, but as she sharpened her focus she thought maybe the shape could be trees. Where there were trees there was water and where there was water there might be a house.

Charlotte picked up her bags again and followed the trail south. The dual track had definitely been worn down by wagon wheels, but still the hem of her long skirt rustled the tall grass down the middle with every step.

Finally, she spotted a tendril of smoke on the horizon. Anticipation swelled in her chest. It was the only sign of a homestead she'd seen since leaving Hollister. As she climbed the slight rise she could see the tops of trees clumped together in a line that followed the horizon. A structure began to take shape and separate itself from the tree-lined backdrop. Charlotte's system flooded with relief. As she drew closer, she slowed her pace, searching for any signs of life.

Charlotte wasn't sure what she'd expected, but this tiny cottage on the frontier was still a surprise. This was what it meant to carve something from nothing. And from the looks of the place, whoever lived here needed help. Or possibly no one had lived there for a while. It was actually hard to know for sure.

She rotated slowly and watched for someone who might be approaching the house, but only saw two horses grazing near an open barn that looked more like a lean-to, half sod, half wood. Animals residing on the place was definitely an indication that someone resided in the rustic cabin.

Charlotte pushed the door of the cabin open with the side of her bag just enough to peek inside.

"Hello?"

She hadn't expected anyone, but it seemed wise to announce herself anyway. Once inside the dark interior, her optimism waned. The place looked as if no one lived in it. Or if someone did live in this place they had suffered something tragic.

There were small clods of dirt and debris all over the floor of the main living area, which doubled as both kitchen, dining, and sitting area. Although there were none of the comforts of a traditional dwelling. From her position just inside the front door she could see that there were two small beds in rooms separated by a partial wall and blankets hung from rope strung across each opening. There was a disheveled blanket on one bed, while the other was neatly made, as if it hadn't been slept in. That struck her as curious.

Random dishware sat on the kitchen table and along the shelves near the sink. Cups on their sides, bowls turned over. There were a few odd pieces of clothing hanging on a hook near the fireplace. The fire had long ago died down, but when she held out her hand there was warmth so someone had been here at some point. The room with the made bed also had an overturned crate as a bedside table, along with a rustic chest with three drawers.

She set her two bags near the front door.

There was an organized pile of wood by the hearth. She stirred the coals until she found some life and then added a few woodchips to get things going. Then she added a couple of small sticks of wood. She lifted the lid of the black pot hanging beside the fire. It looked like gruel or porridge long past being edible. She dropped the lid, swung the pot away from the fire, and walked back to the door. What she really needed was water. Chickens scuttled out of her way as she crossed the dirt between the cabin and the well. She lowered the bucket, but her arms were so worn out from carrying her luggage for so long that she could barely haul it up once it was full of water. Her muscles twitched from fatigue. Only the desperation of her thirst gave her the strength to hoist the bucket up and over the edge of the well. She scooped water into her hands and drank. Then she splashed water on the side of her face and wiped at the dried blood with her skirt. She was a wreck.

Charlotte left the bucket of water on the ground and staggered back to the house. She just needed to rest for a little while and figure out what to do next.

CHAPTER NINE

W es sank her fingers in the dirt on the far side of the plowed field and then closed her fingers around it. She raised her closed fist to her face and inhaled the scent of rich earth.

It smelled like home.

Since losing her brother she'd tried to refocus on the good things—every small thing that could bring her joy.

Wes straightened and arched her back into a stretch. She surveyed the planted field, feeling proud that their work was beginning to pay off.

She shouldered the rifle and headed toward the tree line. Wes figured she'd try to do a little hunting before dark. With any luck, she'd find something. She traipsed out away from the plowed field, past the old cottonwood that guarded Clyde's grave.

She was casually walking when a covey of quail burst from the tall grass stopping her in her tracks. Wes hadn't been prepared to see something so soon and failed to take aim in time. No matter. She was more in the mood for rabbit.

Wes cut across the prairie toward the creek where there were more trees and the grass thinned along the bank. She found a good spot to sit and watch for movement, resting the heavy Hawken rifle on her lap. Hunting for wild game had always been something she had a knack for even back in Tennessee. She'd use any excuse to avoid being stuck with household chores. Wes would cinch up her dress and head off into the woods for hours at a time. She could sit for quite a while in one spot, waiting, without getting bored. Time in the woods were hours to think and get lost in her own musings.

Nowadays she never wore dresses. She'd long ago abandoned the uniform of her sex for trousers. Wearing her brother's hand-me-down clothes made sense given the hard labor of working the claim.

Something stirred and her attention was called back to the task at hand.

A rabbit appeared at the edge of the tall grass. Its ears twitched and its nose worked at the wind for anything that was amiss. But Wes was downwind so the hare advanced a few yards, nibbling at something on the ground. She exhaled slowly. Her aim was steady and sure as she set the blade sight at the end of the long barrel on the rabbit's head. The set trigger made the slightest noise and the rabbit perked up but didn't run. She squeezed the second trigger.

The rifle discharge echoed loudly in the open landscape. A hundred feet to the east, birds took off in a flurry of wings, dark against the pink of the sunset sky.

Wes picked up the dead animal by its hind feet and started walking back toward the house. The light was fading by the time she reached the edge of the yard.

She leaned the rifle up at the corner of the barn and set about skinning and cleaning the rabbit on a table roughly constructed of a few old boards nailed onto tree stumps. She wiped her hunting knife on her trousers before she slid it back into the sheath at her belt. She'd cut the meat into a stew once she was inside.

❖

The sound of a gunshot woke Charlotte. She blinked and then raised herself up from the bed with one arm. Her skirt was damp and smudged on one side where she'd dried her face earlier. She'd fallen asleep in the tiny bedroom of the cabin and had no idea how long she'd been there. The waning sunlight through the small window told her it was late, but exactly how late she wasn't sure.

She rubbed her eyes with the heels of her palms and for a few minutes sat on the edge of the bed to wait for the fog to leave her brain. Had she really heard the shot or was it simply a bad dream?

A chicken was standing in the open door of the cabin as if to gauge whether she was alive or dead. The bird cocked its head and clucked loudly until Charlotte roused herself enough to scare the creature away. She stumbled around the table near the fireplace in search of something to defend herself with. She needed to pull herself together.

From the tiny window over the sink, she could see a man walking in her direction. He had a rifle and something in his other hand. Even in the dim light she could see that he was carrying something he'd obviously just shot.

Charlotte stood watching until he was almost at the cabin. Now she was more than a little cornered. She could feel her heart's rapid pace and pressed her palm to her chest.

What to do? What to do? She had nowhere to run. When she heard footsteps near the front door she grabbed the only weapon she could think of.

"Don't come any closer!" Charlotte wielded the cast iron skillet like a bat. The man looked up and regarded her with wide eyes. "I'm not afraid to use this."

"This is *my* house." Despite declaring ownership, he took a step back.

He carried a rifle in one hand and the skinned rabbit in the other and he also had an intimidating knife hanging from his belt. Charlotte's frying pan was outmatched, but she was determined to stand her ground. She'd survived one ambush today and wasn't about to fall prey to this one. She simply stood in the doorway and stared. The man stared back. He looked as if he'd seen a ghost and Charlotte realized she probably looked like someone raised from the dead after all that she'd been through.

The man was tall, with broad shoulders and a lean build. She would go as far as to describe him as handsome, although his smooth clean-shaven face indicated he might be young, maybe in his late twenties. He had the sweet delicate features more associated with boyhood. He had brown eyes and dark, disheveled short hair.

Charlotte sensed a sadness he wore like a heavy coat. His clothes hung loosely on his lanky frame and there were smudges of dirt on his shirt sleeves and bloodstains on his trousers, near where the knife hung at his belt.

"I'm not going to hurt you." His voice carried a note of kindness. The man took another step back.

Charlotte slowly lowered her weapon.

"My name is Wesley Holden. People call me Wes." He laid the rifle on the ground and held up his hand as if to say he meant no harm. "This is my place. I live here."

"My name is Charlotte...Charlotte Rose." Exhaustion was catching up with her. Suddenly, the pan was so heavy that she almost dropped it. "There's been an accident."

Wes made a move toward her and she raised the pan again.

"Easy." Wes didn't try to reach for her. "You just seemed like you were about to topple over."

Wes focused on Charlotte as she lowered the pan once more. Charlotte was watching Wes intently, sizing her up. Beneath the smudges on her face and her hair, Charlotte was still very pretty. She was attractive in a girlish way, with red hair and fair complexion. Wild strands of her hair had slipped loose from the clasp at her neck and swirled around her elegant jawline in the draft from the open door. Her dress was long-sleeved; the bodice was tastefully designed not to show too much. It fit snugly across her breasts and torso down to a sash around her waist. Below the bodice, the folds of her skirt reached the floor. Her skirts rustled when she stepped closer to the threshold. It was only after she moved into the light from the door that Wes could see that her eyes were green.

It was obvious that something terrible had happened to Charlotte. The hem of her dress was dark and torn in places, and there was a smudge of dust and blood on the side of her face. Regardless, she was beautiful and completely out of place in the rustic cabin. Like the solitary rose in a thorn bush.

"What sort of accident?"

"The stage was—"

Wes lunged forward and caught Charlotte with one arm just before she slumped to the floor. Wes gently lowered her to the ground and then laid the rabbit she'd been holding onto the table.

She wiped her hands on a towel and then returned to Charlotte's side. Wes stood for a minute looking down at her. Finally, she decided the only option was to move Charlotte to the bed. She slid her arm under Charlotte's knees and the other under her shoulders. When she got to her feet, Charlotte's head rolled against her shoulder. Strands of her long hair tickled Wes's cheek. She settled Charlotte onto the bed and then went to get water and a cloth.

She pulled a chair close to the bed and dabbed the side of Charlotte's face gently with the damp cloth. There was a bloody crease at her temple. Wes gently moved strands of hair away from it with her fingertips and tried to remove the dried blood.

How in the world did Charlotte end up at her cabin? What was a woman doing traveling alone in the territory? She was either extremely brave or extremely foolish, or perhaps both.

Charlotte's eyes jerked open and she raised her hand, swatting the cloth away.

"What are you doing?" Charlotte blinked rapidly. She seemed confused.

"You're hurt." Wes abruptly stood and stepped back.

Charlotte touched her temple. It ached still. She tried to raise up on her elbow but sank back. Wes was looking at her as if he doubted she was real. How long had it been since this man had seen a woman? Where was she anyway?

"How did I get here?"

"You walked, I think."

"Not here. I meant, how did I get into this bed?" She didn't mean the question to sound as harsh as it came out, but she was scared and sometimes fear made her sound angry. A curse of her Scotch-Irish heritage.

"I...I carried you." Wes seemed self-conscious of his height or his body in general as he stood in the small space. He swept his fingers through his short hair to push it off his forehead and then crossed his arms as if in defense of some encroachment.

"I'm sorry." Charlotte sensed no imminent threat from Wes, so she allowed herself to relax onto the pillow. Exhaustion was catching up with her again.

"Why don't I make some food. You rest a little, eat, and then we can talk." Wes turned without waiting for a reply as if the matter had been settled.

Charlotte was too tired to argue. And it wasn't like she could help any of those she'd left behind. They were beyond helping. Although, it seemed harsh to simply leave them where they'd fallen.

"Here, maybe you'd like to have this." Wes returned with a blanket. He managed to cover her while still maintaining a safe distance.

"Thank you."

Charlotte swallowed the lump rising in her throat. She'd narrowly escaped death. Her escape plan had failed. Now what was she going to do? Charlotte refocused on the moment at hand. She was here and she was alive. She took a deep breath and closed her eyes.

Charlotte tugged the blanket up to her shoulders and rolled onto her side. A repeated loop of the events of the day ran through her tired brain. Even though she was no longer in motion, her limbs still carried the vibration of the day's journey over the hard-packed rutted road as if the bed itself still traveled. But it wasn't too long before even that sensation faded and sleep found her. Fatigue pulled her into darkness. Despite her best efforts to stay awake and on guard, she drifted off to sounds of Wes in the next room, cooking.

CHAPTER TEN

Wes watched Charlotte for a moment from the foot of the bed. She waited for Charlotte to notice her and stir. When she didn't, Wes touched Charlotte's shoulder lightly. It took a moment for Charlotte to wake up.

"The food is ready." Once Charlotte was fully awake, Wes stepped back to allow her space to get out of the bed.

Wes had prepared a rabbit stew, and from the look of it, Charlotte could really use a hot meal. And frankly, so could she. Wes did what felt natural, or as natural as anything could feel in this sort of situation. Where she came from, when someone was in need, you fed them and gave them shelter.

"Why don't you come sit at the table?"

When someone passed away, people brought food. If unable to feed the soul at least the body could be nourished to sooth the grief. But at the far edge of nowhere, community was spread thin. There'd been no one to help her mourn the loss of her brother. She'd been on her own.

Charlotte looked hungrily toward the steaming pot and nodded.

"I suppose I could eat something. Thank you." Charlotte stood awkwardly by the table.

"If you want to sit I can bring you a bowl," Wes said.

She served them each a bowl of stew and they sat across from each other and ate in silence. Wes's mind was a flurry of unanswered questions. She really had no idea what might happen next, or how this woman had come to be at her cabin injured and unannounced. Wes tried to wait until they'd both had a chance to eat. The food seemed to be having a good effect on Charlotte; she seemed less fragile. Her eyes brightened. The candle in the center of the table cast the room in soft, warm light.

"This is good, thank you." Charlotte smiled for the first time.

"There's more if you like." Wes was feeling unsettled having a stranger in the house, so she wasn't sure her stomach could handle a second serving. Wes found that she could hardly make eye contact with Charlotte, looking down at her lap, or at the fire, or literally anywhere but at Charlotte for fear that under closer inspection, she'd be found out.

Charlotte glanced down at her nearly empty bowl for a moment and Wes took the opportunity to study her. She'd only just met Charlotte, but she seemed spent, worn down from some terrible event. If she had to guess she'd say they were about the same age, but Charlotte might be a little younger. It was hard to tell for sure. Charlotte had a worldly air about her that made Wes want to keep her distance for fear that she'd reveal too much. Clearly, Charlotte thought she was a man and Wes wanted to keep up that appearance. But it was hard to know what Charlotte was thinking. It would be hard to sense anything given the panic coursing through Wes's nervous system at the moment. Charlotte kept looking at her, and it was making the knot in Wes's stomach churn.

Her brother, Clyde, had been Wes's buffer in this new place against the outside world. He'd helped Wes keep her secret. Without him it was going to be hard for Wes to maintain the life she'd worked hard to build. Having an outsider on the place would only complicate things.

"Do you mind if I ask what happened?" The sooner Wes could sort this out the sooner she could get Charlotte on her way back to wherever she belonged.

"I was on the stage from Kansas City to Santa Fe and we were, attacked, or robbed, or..." Charlotte paused, her brow furrowed as if she were thinking hard to remember. "I'm really not sure."

She waited for Charlotte to continue.

"There were men, riders, with covered faces. I heard them talk to the driver, but I couldn't really hear what they were saying." She took a breath. "Then the men ordered everyone out of the coach." Her hand holding the spoon began to visibly tremble. "Someone fired a shot and then there was another gunshot...and...I woke up on the ground. I'm not sure how much time passed."

"And the others?" Tension ratchetted up in Wes's system. Drifters had been stealing cattle and ransacking untended claims. Or so she'd heard from Wade Miller, the owner of the mercantile in Hollister. She should probably start carrying her rifle out to the field with her for protection.

"No one survived."

Charlotte's haunted expression tugged at Wes's heart. She had the unfamiliar urge to protect Charlotte from harm. But then she remembered where she was and *who* she was.

"You can't stay here." Wes blurted out the one coherent thought that kept circling in her head. Charlotte absolutely could not stay. She would see Wes for who she was, and everything would be ruined. She was sorry for Charlotte's hardship, but it wasn't her problem to solve.

"I don't plan to stay here." There was frustration and defensiveness in Charlotte's statement.

"I didn't mean to upset you." Wes didn't want to seem callous. She tried to imagine herself in a similar situation. "I'll take you to Hollister as soon as you feel up to it. And then you can be on your way to wherever you were headed."

"California." Charlotte sounded a bit defeated.

Charlotte let the wooden spoon sink in her uneaten stew. To her credit, she hadn't started crying. Wes didn't know how she'd deal with it if Charlotte became emotional.

"I'm sorry." Wes tried to soften her words. It wasn't Charlotte's fault that any of this had happened. "I didn't mean to imply you'd done anything wrong." She paused and met Charlotte's gaze for an instant. "It just isn't possible for you to stay here."

"I understand." Charlotte seemed resigned to her fate. At least she didn't argue.

"You can stay the night." Wes looked down at the table as she spoke. "I'll sleep in the barn. And then I'll take you to Hollister tomorrow."

"There's no need for you to sleep in the barn."

"It wouldn't be right for an unmarried fella to sleep in here… with you." Keeping up appearances and putting some physical distance between them would hopefully buy her some time. She folded her hands on the table and focused on keeping her tone stern. But she still didn't look at Charlotte. Charlotte's gaze cut right through her and she wasn't sure why. Wes needed to shore up her cover in front of this stranger. Charlotte could ruin everything without even trying.

CHAPTER ELEVEN

Charlotte watched Wes from the window, barely visible in the lantern light as he walked toward the barn. After they'd eaten the evening meal, he'd hurriedly gathered blankets for his bed in the barn and then couldn't get out of the house fast enough. Wes was like a skittish colt.

There was something different about Wes, but Charlotte couldn't quite bring the reason into focus. He seemed withdrawn, on edge, and angry that Charlotte was here. But it wasn't like she'd planned to get shot at and left for dead. That hadn't been part of her plan at all.

She sat by the fire lost in thought for a while, mesmerized by the glowing embers. Still tired from her ordeal, she decided to do the best she could with what was offered and settle in for the night.

Darkness had descended on the cabin quickly. Charlotte drew the quilt curtain that separated her sleeping space from the main room across the rope line in order to have privacy. A single tallow candle lit the small bedroom as she slipped out of her dress and into a long nightgown. At first, she was self-conscious about undressing in a strange house. But then she remembered how Wes could hardly look at her, let alone remain in the same room with her, so she relaxed and changed quickly out of her garments.

It wasn't until she had removed her dress and got a better look at it that she realized what a state she'd been in when she arrived. Her dress was a mess. It needed to be washed and mended before she could even wear it again. She took a moment to examine her hands. There were smudges of dirt on the back of her hands and her nails were darkened with dried blood. No wonder Wes could hardly stand to look at her.

There was a basin of water near the hearth. Charlotte retrieved it and brought it back to the bedroom so that she could wash up a bit. She took the clasp from her hair and brushed out the tangles. The mundane bedtime ritual soothed her frayed nerves and helped her relax a little.

Before settling into bed, curiosity made her want to examine the rustic chest of drawers in the corner of the small room. She set the candle holder on top and opened the top drawer. There was a letter addressed to someone named Clyde Holden. A shirt lay on the other side of the drawer, folded haphazardly. She gently lifted the shirt and held it to her face. The cloth smelled of cedar and smoke and fresh air. Was this what Wes smelled like? Who was Clyde? Was this Clyde's room rather than Wes's?

She had lots of questions. She considered looking in the other two drawers, but the blankets called to her. She closed the drawer and carried the candle back to the upturned crate beside the narrow bed.

The evening air was cool, but she left the window shutter ajar so that she could hear the night sounds of this new world. The crickets she recognized, but there were otherworldly sounds too. The world outside her window was alive with nocturnal activity. The eerie cry of a coyote made the skin on her arms pebble. She quickly closed the shutter and set the bar across it.

She sat back on the bed and drew her knees to her chest, feeling very alone all of a sudden. Regardless of what she thought she'd find at the end of her journey in California, traveling through the unsettled territory had possibly been a huge mistake.

❖

Wes arranged fresh hay in the back of the barn as a makeshift mattress and spread a blanket over the top of it. Once she'd set her boots aside, she lay on the blanket and pulled a second one up to her chin. Her horse, Dusty, glanced over at her as if to ask if she was lost. The short answer was yes. She'd allowed herself to be cast out of her own cabin by a total stranger.

There was no way she could sleep inside under the same roof as Charlotte. What could Charlotte know? Nothing, that's what. And Wes intended to keep it that way.

There was no reason for Charlotte to linger. First thing in the morning she'd saddle the horses and carry her back to Hollister so that she could catch the stagecoach back to wherever she was going. She was certain that Charlotte would agree to this plan.

Wes closed her eyes and tried her best to relax, but despite her exhaustion she was all wrought up. Her thoughts were running in circles making her even more tired but not allowing her to give in to sleep.

Her tired brain began to return to times past, to her childhood in the Tennessee hills.

One of the first things she'd learned as a child was her name and where she lived. Her sense of belonging was tied to place, to home. But without her parents, home had become something that was no longer the same. Home had become family instead of a place, and her family was her brother, Clyde. What did all of that mean now without him? She'd left what passed for home behind and she'd left her name too. Well, not completely, but she'd definitely become a different person on the journey. The few folks who knew her didn't know the person she was in the before time. Could she truly belong here on her own, on her own terms without Clyde?

Wes took a deep breath and let it out slowly.

She opened her eyes and stared at the rafters overhead. There was no way to answer all these questions at the moment. She needed to refocus her mind. She began to silently repeat an old hymn that had been one of her mother's favorites. As a child, she remembered her mother singing it while hanging linens to dry. And then of course she'd heard it sung during Sunday service for years after that. But it was her mother's version she remembered. The way she'd half hum and half sing so that it was hard for Wes to make out the words. But in times of turmoil, or fear, remembering the tune soothed her.

She hummed to herself.

Wes hummed the tune over and over until she felt her pulse slow to a normal rate and the throbbing tension at the back of her neck eased. She took another deep breath and let it out, rolled onto her side, and gave in to sleep. Tomorrow things would get better. Tomorrow Charlotte would leave and she'd get back to working the farm.

❖

Wes was floating. She sensed her body surrounded by water. She remembered what it felt like to wade into the swimming hole in the summertime. She'd stay in the water for so long that her feet would go numb from the cold. A shiver ran through her body. Wes jerked awake, confused by her surroundings.

Thunder clapped loudly. Large drops of water found their way through the thatched barn roof. A sluice of water and mud flowed past her makeshift straw mattress. Her trousers were soaked to the knees and one of her boots had been swept along and was filling with water.

"Damn!" Wes scrambled to save her boot from the deluge. She turned it over and muddy water sloshed out.

She hopped on one soggy sock-covered foot and then the other as she tried to tug on her wet boots.

Lightning flashed and a low rumble followed. Then another flash and a loud boom that sounded much closer. Rain was coming down in sheets. She wrapped a blanket around her head and shoulders and made a mad dash through the darkness toward the cabin.

Wes expected Charlotte to be asleep, but she wasn't. When Wes burst through the door, breathing hard from her sprint through the downpour, Charlotte was up, stirring the fire.

Wes had a vision, a flash of some future image of Charlotte by the fire. Although Wes was absolutely certain that Charlotte should leave, the vision was as sharp as a lightning strike. When she saw Charlotte, it was like she'd seen her there a thousand times before and would see her a thousand times again, standing by the hearth as if she'd always been there and was meant to be there. As if her soul recognized some connection from a past or future she'd only just now remembered. The sensation was so strong it caused her to sway on her feet. She braced her hand against the doorframe to steady herself.

"Are you alright?" Charlotte straightened and regarded Wes with a curious expression.

"I'm fine." Wes tried to sound as if she was. "Water was comin' in the barn pretty bad and I—"

"Oh, you're soaked." Charlotte moved a chair closer to the fireplace. "Come sit here until you dry."

Charlotte was wearing a nightgown and had one of the blankets from the bed wrapped around herself like a shawl. Her hair had been loosed and it curled in waves across her shoulders. She seemed to realize she wasn't fully dressed and pulled the blanket more tightly, holding it closed with both hands.

"Thank you." Wes left wet footprints all the way to the hearth to take a seat. She held her chilled fingers out to the fire to warm them. She realized that her wet clothing was clinging to her chest, and even in the low light from the fire might reveal more than she'd intended.

Charlotte was standing behind her and jumped when Wes got to her feet. Charlotte was standing so near that she almost bumped into her.

"Sorry." Wes hugged herself. "I should put on some dry clothes."

Charlotte watched Wes draw the quilt in front of his bedroom. He seemed on edge still, even though Charlotte was doing her best not to get in his way or make him feel beholding to her in her hour of need. She certainly wasn't normally a woman who needed to be rescued, but forces had conspired against her. After a few moments, Wes returned to the fire in dry clothes and bare feet.

"Um, I might need to sleep inside after all...if that won't make you uncomfortable." Wes's curt tone from earlier had softened.

"I'm fine with that." Charlotte took a seat near the fire, opposite the chair Wes had been sitting in. "You don't want to get sick from being cold and wet."

They were quiet for a moment, but then Charlotte could contain her curiosity no longer.

"Does someone else live here?"

"Not anymore." Wes stared at the fire without making eye contact.

"Who is Clyde?"

After a long pause, Wes finally answered.

"He is—was my brother."

Charlotte knew from his expression that there was more to this story. But before she could ask, Wes clarified.

"He died a month ago."

"Oh, I'm so sorry." Now some of the sadness that she'd sensed in Wes made sense.

"It was sudden." Wes still didn't look at her.

"What happened?" Charlotte was trying not to push for fear he would shut down. She had so many questions, and it was obvious that Wes's grief was still fresh.

Wes shrugged.

"I don't know exactly. I wasn't with him when it happened. He went out hunting and was thrown from his horse. I didn't find him until the next morning."

How terrible it must have been for Wes to discover his brother dead. Charlotte had witnessed the death of her mother, but that was after a long illness. She'd had time to mentally prepare for the loss. Losing someone so close suddenly was probably hard to deal with, especially in such a remote and lonely place.

They sat quietly for a while, watching the fire before Charlotte finally spoke.

"How long have you lived here?"

"Hmm." He had to think about it. "Five years, maybe a little longer."

"I'm so sorry for your loss." She didn't know what else to say.

"Weren't your fault." Wes sniffed and wiped his face with his sleeve.

Was he crying? Charlotte wasn't used to seeing a man reveal so much emotion. Her heart ached for Wes, and it was hard not to reach out to comfort him, but his body language told her that would not be welcomed.

The rain was suddenly heavy. Huge droplets pelted the roof as if a gale had blown in. The wind sounded angry and disturbed. The cabin was dark except for the firelight, which cast Wes's shadow against the rough-hewn log wall behind him. Charlotte was about to ask another question when the door blew open and banged loudly. Rain and wind rushed into the warm interior, soaking the floor around the doorway.

Wes leapt from his chair and swung the door shut and put the bar in place across it. He wrung water from his hands and then swept his fingers through his damp hair. Charlotte realized that she was locked in with him, for better or worse, to weather the storm. She wasn't afraid of him. In fact, she felt safe around Wes, which was a curious thing to note.

"The wind is really churning up out there." He returned to his chair.

They sat quietly for a few minutes as the storm raged outside.

"Will the horses be okay?" She wasn't sure how weatherproof the barn was.

"They might spook, but they'll be alright."

Wes turned to look at her for the first time. The glow from the flames made orange highlights in his dark eyes. His gaze was so intense that she had to look away. Charlotte feared that under his focus she might not measure up.

"What made you come here?" That was the first real question he'd asked her.

Charlotte considered how best to respond.

"There were many reasons." That was the truth without being too specific. "I suppose I wanted a different life."

"Different than what?" He seemed like he really wanted to know.

"I've been working as a maid at a hotel in St. Louis. And I suppose after seeing so many others follow their dreams for a better life out west, I wanted a chance for that too."

"Weren't you worried to travel by yourself?"

"Yes, but what other choice did I have?" Charlotte paused, considering how much detail she wanted to share about being romanced and abandoned by Nathaniel. "I did have someone, but that didn't work out. He left a ticket and I decided to use it."

"But what were you going to do once you got where you were going? Do you have people there?" Wes seemed to be trying to figure out some sort of puzzle.

"I supposed I hadn't thought everything through completely. I can see that now." Charlotte thought of Nathaniel and how wrong she'd been. She thought of all the people she'd known who'd disappointed her. And after everything, she'd ended up on the far edge of nowhere at the mercy of a total stranger. Life never seemed to stop throwing obstacles her way. She followed one impulsive decision with another, and now, here she was.

"What if things didn't work out when you got there, wherever you were going?"

"California?" Charlotte couldn't help being amused by her cavalier attitude about the harshness of life. "I suppose all I was looking for was a little kindness and a fresh start."

Wes turned his attention back to the fire. He wasn't looking at her when he spoke.

"Well, I hope you find it." But he didn't sound very confident that she would.

The rain came in waves, but the lightning seemed to have gone. Charlotte was sleepy and didn't think she could stay awake any longer. She covered a yawn with her hand.

"You should get some rest. I'll sit up a while." Wes was looking at her again with those soulful eyes.

"Are you sure?"

"Yeah. I haven't been sleeping much lately." That explained the dark shadows under his eyes.

Charlotte nodded. She paused as she walked past his chair. She hesitated but then lightly touched his shoulder. "Thank you."

❖

Charlotte's touch left a heat signature on Wes's shoulder. What was Charlotte thanking her for? She was frozen in place as Charlotte's footsteps softly receded behind her. It wasn't until the bedframe creaked in the adjacent room that Wes realized she'd been holding her breath. She closed her eyes and exhaled. That small brush of human contact and kindness cast in stark relief the ache of loneliness in her chest. She squeezed her eyes shut, but the tears came anyway. Wes buried her face in the crook of her arm to muffle the sound. The rain had eased, and the last thing she wanted was for Charlotte to hear her crying.

The surge of emotion caught her by surprise. Not the crying part, but the other part. This had nothing to do with losing Clyde. This was something deeper. A feeling she'd never allowed herself—desire— the desire for more. Wes wasn't even sure what that encompassed, and until she'd arrived at the edge of the frontier she hadn't even dreamed she could actually have the sort of life she wanted. But hearing Charlotte talk about her own hopes brought things up for Wes too. She was lonely even before losing her brother. Wes hardly allowed herself to admit that, but it was true. She had the farm and her independence, but was that enough?

Wes straightened in her chair, braced her palms on her thighs, and tried to pull herself together. Yes, Charlotte had touched her just now. But Charlotte had no real idea of who Wes truly was and she never would. Wes knew that could never be. Charlotte could never be her friend because once Charlotte knew the truth everything would be over. There was no way Wes could allow that to happen.

She stepped into her room and slid the blanket across the opening so that she could get ready for bed.

When she'd first come in from the barn, Wes had put on a Henley undershirt, with buttons at the neck underneath her outer shirt. But beneath all of that, the wrapping to cover her breasts was still damp. She untied the cloth and slowly unwound the damp cotton strips of fabric and hung them over the end of the bed to dry.

She retrieved a nightshirt from the foot of her bed and slipped it over her head. She settled under the covers and listened to the rain. It was hard to sleep knowing that Charlotte was in the next room.

CHAPTER TWELVE

The smell of food cooking woke Wes. She shifted on the bed and yawned. She'd actually slept for the first time in days. Maybe for the first time since losing her brother. Wes sat on the edge of the bed and rolled her head from side to side to stretch her neck muscles.

Her nightshirt had gotten all twisted. She adjusted her shirt and smoothed the front of it with her hands and then remembered that she wasn't alone in the house. She quickly applied the wrapping around her chest and tugged on the shirt she'd worn the previous night. She finger combed her hair a bit.

When she slid the quilt aside, she saw Charlotte near the fireplace. She'd changed into a clean dress. The shoulders and hem of her dress were damp, as was her hair. She smiled at Wes.

"I hope you don't mind. I went out to see if there were any eggs and found a few. I thought breakfast might be nice." She straightened from her task and turned to face Wes. "I made biscuits too."

Wes saw that Charlotte had used the iron skillet with a lid and sunk it into the coals.

"Smells good." If Charlotte thought cooking was going to make Wes let her stay, she was mistaken. But there was no harm in being polite. And besides, Wes had woken up hungry.

Wes opened the front door and looked out. It was still very early. A line of pink-tinted clouds sat near the horizon. The rain had mostly stopped, although an angry dark cloud hovered to the east in the direction of Hollister. She hurried to the privy, and when she returned to the house she washed up quickly in a basin near the sink, splashing cold water on her face to chase away the cobwebs of sleep.

She returned to the table unsure of what to do. It was strange to have someone else doing things like cooking in her cabin.

Charlotte set a tin plate of eggs and biscuits in front of her. Wes took a seat and waited for Charlotte to join her. There was coffee too. Charlotte poured two steaming mugs. This was like a breakfast for kings. Wes hadn't taken time to gather eggs in two weeks. She did come across broken eggs probably scavenged by raccoons, but she'd had none for herself.

"Did you sleep well?" Charlotte asked.

Wes already had a mouthful of food, so she simply nodded. She figured they'd eat and then leave for Hollister. The sooner Charlotte was on her way, the better.

They sat without talking for a few moments until Charlotte abruptly set her fork down. There was a stricken expression on her face. Charlotte covered her mouth with her hand and looked at Wes with wide eyes, then dashed for the door. Wes was so taken by surprise that she sat for a few seconds before following.

Charlotte braced with one arm at the corner of the cabin and heaved what little breakfast she'd eaten.

"Are you alright?" Wes asked from a respectful distance.

Charlotte waved her off.

After a moment or two, Charlotte straightened. She'd had a cloth tucked into her waist from cooking. She pulled it free and covered her mouth. Charlotte kept one hand on the wall as she walked back to the door. Rain had started again.

"Are you sick?" Wes knew her question was edged with worry. She couldn't very well take Charlotte to Hollister on horseback or even by wagon if she were ill.

"I don't think I'm sick." Charlotte sat down again. She slid her plate aside, braced her elbows on the table and covered her face with her hands. "It must just be nerves from everything that happened yesterday."

That was certainly plausible. Charlotte seemed well otherwise. Wes took her seat. She'd been so hungry that she'd wolfed her breakfast down. Only a small bite of biscuit remained on her plate.

Charlotte looked at Wes for what seemed like forever before she spoke.

"Oh no." Charlotte's expression was hard to interpret. Was she sad or frightened or both? Once again, she jumped up and ran outside.

This time, Wes didn't follow. After a few minutes, Charlotte returned to her seat.

As if on cue, thunder rumbled, and then heavy rain began to pelt the roof. Wes shut the door again to block the wind and rain. The dark cloud she'd seen in the east had arrived.

Wes began to pace. After a minute, she looked at Charlotte still seated at the table.

"There's no way to get to Hollister today anyway." Wes could tell Charlotte still didn't feel well. "Not with the storm and all."

Charlotte looked up at Wes. His expression softened. Charlotte was puzzled by her sudden sickness and didn't think she could ride a horse while nauseous anyway so she appreciated his consideration for her condition and the weather.

"Maybe I should lie down." She'd made it this far. And she wasn't going to allow her dream of a life in California to be derailed by an ambush. But for now, she needed to rest and regain her strength. "I can clean this up later." She motioned toward the dishes on the table as she stood.

"Don't worry about it." Wes seemed bothered by the suggestion for some reason. "I can take care of this."

Charlotte was in no condition to argue. She slowly walked back to the bedroom, drew the draped quilt, and lay on her side. She willed her stomach to settle. She'd gotten sick two days ago as well, for no reason. She'd had to dash from the boarding house and out to the privy first thing in the morning. She hadn't even eaten breakfast, so she couldn't blame the food. In truth, simply the smell of meat frying had sent her stomach into upheaval and she'd barely made it outside before becoming ill.

Oh, no. A horrible thought occurred to her. She fisted the blanket and held it to her mouth. When was the last time she'd had her monthly cycle? She backtracked in her mind. It had been at least eight weeks. It had been exactly eight weeks since she'd last seen Nathaniel.

No, no, no.

Anxiety filled her with dread, but she chided herself not to jump to conclusions. A missed cycle didn't mean anything. She hadn't been eating or sleeping well. She'd been so upset about how Nathaniel had treated her that she honestly hadn't been taking care of herself. And now the rigors of travel and the ambush had caught up with her. That was it and nothing more. But deep down she worried. Rain pelted the roof as she huddled under the blankets and tried not to panic.

❖

Wes sat at the table and listened to the rain. She stared at the quilt drawn across the opening to Clyde's room and allowed her mind to remember Charlotte's hand on her shoulder. A warm sensation settled in her stomach.

At some point she noticed that the angle of the light through the window had shifted. It was midday or early afternoon, she wasn't sure. She'd let her mind wander.

The fire had long ago died and only the smallest glowing embers could be found when she stirred the coals. She added kindling and then a couple of larger sticks of wood to the growing blaze so that she could boil some coffee. She focused on an imperfection in the log wall near the fire and allowed her eyes to lose focus while she waited for the kettle to boil.

Wes had been feeling a bit like the walking dead, barely aware of herself or her surroundings. The weight of loss gathered around her like a suffocating blanket, heavy and dark.

Whatever happened to someone when they died, they for sure left their physical body behind. She knew without a doubt that Clyde was no longer with her, the minute she'd touched his hand.

Ben Caufield had been by once. But she hadn't seen anyone else since the day she'd laid Clyde to rest. Charlotte showing up the way she did was probably a blessing in disguise. It was a reminder that there was a world out there, even though Wes sometimes didn't feel as if she was part of it.

She'd just poured a cup of coffee for herself when she heard Charlotte moving about.

"I made coffee if you'd like some." Wes held a cup up as Charlotte stepped into the room.

"No thanks." Charlotte shook her head.

"How are you feeling?"

"Better, thank you."

Charlotte was beginning to see Wes in a new way. He seemed more at ease as he sipped coffee and watched the weather out the window. Wes did have an easy confidence that inspired Charlotte to relax. He wasn't the sort of man that demanded attention or made unwanted advances. At least, not so far. Charlotte had to remind herself not to romanticize the situation. All men were basically the same, all men wanted the same things. Especially from women. Hadn't she just learned that the hard way?

"I was thinking that we should probably let someone know where you are."

"What?" Charlotte had been lost in thought.

"Well, if someone found the stagecoach, or if it doesn't arrive in Santa Fe when it's supposed to, won't someone be looking for you?"

"No one was expecting me there, but I suppose the stage company does keep records of who purchases tickets." Charlotte hadn't given it much thought. She'd been too concerned with her own survival. "Or at the very least they must keep track of how many passengers each coach carries."

Wes studied her for a moment.

"I'm going to ride out and take a look." He drained the last of his coffee. "The rain has eased a bit."

She was afraid he might suggest also taking her into Hollister. Charlotte was in no hurry to leave. She needed time to think and sort out her situation.

"You probably shouldn't be out in the weather if you're not feeling well." Wes pulled on a thin cloth jacket, then reached for his hat and the rifle.

Charlotte felt herself relax at the suggestion that she should remain behind.

"You walked south from the main road?" Wes turned to look at her before crossing the threshold.

She didn't remember telling him, but the trail to his cabin was the only turnoff she'd seen. Charlotte nodded.

"I was walking back toward Hollister when I saw the cutoff." She still couldn't believe she'd been lucky enough to find a safe haven in such a remote place.

Wes noticed Charlotte's expression change the minute she'd suggested that Charlotte should stay a while longer. Charlotte probably just needed a bit more rest. She'd obviously been through a harrowing ordeal. Wes's departure was as much about taking a look at what had transpired as it was about needing to be away from Charlotte. Not that she doubted the truth of Charlotte's story. Drifters and local native tribes were always a threat.

"Put the bar over the door when I leave." Wes turned up the collar of her coat to shield herself from the light rain still falling. "I'll be back before dark."

Wes slogged through the wet grass toward the barn. Clyde's horse, Ned, was standing close to Dusty, probably as much for warmth as for a shield from the wind-driven rain. It was still spring and the weather could be warm in the full sun of midday, but rain and wind brought a chill back to the air. With hardly any features on this open landscape to block the weather, the wind could be strong and had quite a bite when it was cold.

She saddled Dusty, slid her rifle into its sheath attached near the horn, and then swung onto the saddle with one swift motion. Wes guided Dusty out of the barn toward the trail and then turned north. It felt good to be outside. Sharing close quarters with Charlotte was a bit stressful. She'd been careful not to reveal her secret, but with Charlotte so near it would only be a matter of time. Wes needed to help Charlotte get to wherever she was going, anywhere but here.

The light rain didn't let up.

After riding for an hour or so, the shoulders of Wes's coat were soaked. Water dripped from the brim of her hat. Every bit of her clothing was getting more soaked by the minute. Maybe she should have waited longer to leave. The sky had brightened a little so maybe the clouds were beginning to break up.

She didn't have to ride very far once she hit the main trail. The shape of the coach stood out amongst the sameness of the prairie. Wes was a little surprised that no one had shown up to claim it, but then again, the attack or whatever it was had only happened the previous day. It might take longer than that for anyone on either end of the route to realize there'd been a problem. Wes had no clear idea of the stage schedule. She'd never had the money in hand to ride it, which made her wonder how Charlotte had come to have a ticket. The price of a ticket from St. Louis to Santa Fe had to be expensive.

The door of the coach was ajar. She didn't dismount, but instead, peeked inside from the saddle. Charlotte had said the other passengers had been shot. There were no bodies now. There were bullet holes in the wooden walls of the carriage, and someone had obviously shot a flaming arrow into the interior. The seating area was partially burned, but probably the heavy rain from earlier dowsed it.

Bullet holes and arrows made it hard to know who had done what. Either way, Charlotte was very lucky to be alive. Things could have gone much worse for her. The fact that Charlotte hadn't been taken made Wes assume this had been a robbery gone wrong and that the arrow was an afterthought. Nothing more than a message, a reminder, for white settlers.

Wes studied the ground. There were lots of hoofprints, a few coyote prints, and maybe even a wagon. The rain had erased some of the details, but it seemed like someone had headed south, cutting across the open field. If they'd headed south then that meant they might come across her place. Wes's heart rate ratchetted up a notch. She'd left Charlotte alone without a weapon.

"Come on, Dusty!" She pressed the heels of her boots into his sides and swiftly turned him south. They set off at a fast clip through the tall grass.

When they reached the tree line, Wes slowed Dusty's pace. Trees clustered in a narrow grove along the creek. If the riders crossed the creek and kept heading west, then she'd stop worrying. Wes studied the prints in the mud as Dusty wove through the trees. A gunshot surprised her. Dusty flinched and so did she. Wes tightened her grip on the reins and intently scanned the area. She didn't see anyone. The whoosh of an arrow narrowly missed her. She urged Dusty to run. Whatever was happening, she'd ended up in the middle of it. Before she could take cover deeper in the grove, she felt a sharp pain in her left arm, but she kept moving. Stopping was not an option.

Wes rode south for a half hour or so. The gunfire was definitely moving west. It was distant and sporadic now. She turned east, cutting across the open prairie in a diagonal to get back to the farm. Blood had soaked her shirtsleeve, her jacket, and trickled down onto Dusty. An arrow protruded from her upper arm, just below her shoulder.

It was dusk by the time she reached the cabin. The open door cast a rectangle of soft light on the ground from the fireplace like an invitation, welcoming her home. She should have been glad, but her first thought was worry.

❖

Charlotte heard something outside the cabin and rushed to the door. Wes eased out of the saddle and leaned against Dusty for a moment. The light was fading fast, but even still, Charlotte could see that something was wrong. Wes turned to face her. Only then did she see the staff of the arrow coming from Wes's upper arm.

"I told you to bar the door." Wes sounded angry.

"I did bar the door. But then it got late and I was worried." Charlotte touched the sleeve of Wes's coat. It was wet from rain and blood. "You're soaked and hurt."

"Yeah…wrong place, wrong time." With one hand, Wes tied Dusty to a post railing near the front door.

"What do you mean?"

"If they'd meant to kill me, I'd be dead." Wes staggered toward the cabin steps. "I followed tracks from where your stage was attacked. I was afraid they were coming here."

"I haven't seen anyone all day except you." She followed Wes inside. The thought that she might have found herself in the middle of some retaliatory action sent a wave of panic through her system. But she tried to calm down and focus on the crisis right in front of her instead of worrying about the *what ifs*. "Sit down and let me take a look at that."

"Okay." Wes seemed in shock a little. He was slumped against the table with his injured arm drooping by his side. Watery red droplets ran down his fingers onto the floor.

Charlotte tugged at the coat collar, heavy with rain but then realized the arrow had obviously gone through both the coat and his shirt. She paused to reassess.

"What are you doing?" Wes snapped out of his stupor and glared at her.

"We need to get you out of these wet clothes so I can look at your arm."

"No." Wes lurched to his feet but swayed and had to drop back to the chair. He covered his face with his right hand and pinched the bridge of his nose.

"We're not going to be able to take this off anyway." Charlotte stepped in front of him so she could see his face more clearly. "I think I'm going to need to cut the sleeve away to get to it."

Wes nodded. He visibly relaxed now that she wasn't trying to help him out of his clothing. She understood his reluctance, but this seemed like an emergency situation in which normal, proper decorum between the sexes might be ignored.

"I will patch this for you later." Charlotte used Wes's hunting knife to cut the fabric and then ripped it further with her hands. Once the cloth was torn from around the entry point, she then slid the lower section of his coat sleeve off. Then she did the same with his shirt sleeve. Wes's arm was leanly muscled. There were old scars on his forearm. She wondered about them, but didn't ask.

The arrow had gone through the muscle of Wes's upper arm. The arrowhead had come through the flesh and extended on the other side by several inches. Now that Charlotte could clearly see the wound, she paused, unsure of what to do next.

"You'll need to break it and pull it the rest of the way through." Wes spoke without looking at her. He was clenching his other fist and staring at the fireplace.

"What?" She wasn't sure she understood.

"Break the staff and then pull it through the rest of the way." Wes turned and gazed up at her with a wounded expression. His hair was still damp, and dark wet tendrils clung to his forehead.

"How can I break this?" She wasn't sure she was strong enough.

"Use my knife." He handed it to her again, handle first. "Score it…notch it so that it'll be easier to break."

Charlotte did as he directed, but every time she applied pressure to the wooden shaft Wes winced with pain. The point of entry started to bleed from the movement as she tried to create a notch.

"Okay, I think this is as much as I can do." She was standing over Wes seated in the chair. "Shall I try and break it now?"

He nodded.

Given her proximity, most men would have probably touched her, but Wes seemed uncomfortable with the physical closeness.

"Hand me one of those wooden spoons." Wes pointed toward a utensil at the other end of the table. Charlotte had made food for them and set the table, but that was all before the discovery that Wes was injured.

Wes held the handle of the spoon between his teeth and nodded for her to continue. Charlotte did her best to try to break the wooden shaft without putting too much pressure on the wound, but she was afraid she failed. To Wes's credit, he didn't cry out, but he did pound the table once with his fist and wince.

Relief flooded her system when the shaft cracked loudly. Okay, step one had been accomplished. Now for the hard part.

"Are you ready?" Charlotte gripped the arrowhead with one hand and braced her other hand against Wes's shoulder. "Here we go—"

Wes gripped the edge of the table as Charlotte yanked the broken rod from his arm. He spit the spoon out and slumped back in the chair. Blood was streaming down his arm now.

"You should probably cauterize it."

"How?"

"Use the knife blade. Heat it in the coals and then press it to each opening. It'll stop the bleeding and seal the wound."

"I'm not sure I can do that." Just the thought of hot metal against Wes's skin made her woozy.

"It'll hurt like hell, but it's better to do it now." Wes looked up at her and visibly swallowed. She wondered if he was feeling woozy as well.

Deep down, Charlotte knew he was right, even though she wasn't sure she could go through with it without fainting. She sunk the knife blade into the fire and waited. When the blade was glowing hot, she carried it back to Wes but hesitated.

"Here, I'll do it."

"Are you sure?"

"Yeah. Give it to me before it cools." Wes placed the wooden spoon handle between his teeth again and held out his right hand.

Charlotte heard the slight sizzle and Wes groaned, but she didn't see any of it. She'd turned away at the last second. She was quite taken with Wes's bravery. He'd done this incredibly hard and painful thing without the slightest complaint or hesitation.

The knife made a light thud on the table so that she knew it was safe to turn around. Wes seemed spent. The bleeding had stopped, but in its place was an angry red mark from the hot knife blade.

She quickly set about cleaning the blood from around the wound and took a clean cloth from her bag in the bedroom and tied it around his arm. Then, using thin strips of cloth, she fashioned a sling and helped Wes to adjust his arm so that his wrist rested in the sling. If he could manage not to move his arm for a little while she hoped that would keep the wound from opening up again and give it time to heal a little.

"How does that feel?" She studied Wes's stoic expression.

"Feels okay."

Not the most resounding endorsement of her nursing skills, but she'd take it. At least the arrow hadn't hit bone or other vital organs. If someone had to be pierced by an arrow, this seemed like the best-case scenario. If there was such a thing.

After a few moments, Wes stood up.

"Where are you going?" Charlotte was serving some stewed potatoes into a bowl near the fire.

"I need to go take care of Dusty."

"I'll do it." Charlotte touched Wes's shoulder as if to push him back down into the chair. "You can barely stand."

"Are you sure?" He sounded relieved.

"Quite sure. Just sit right there. Rest and eat some food. I'll be right back." She set a bowl in front of him, touching his shoulder again as she reached past him. If Charlotte was honest with herself she'd admit that she liked being needed.

A lantern was sitting on a shelf near the fireplace. Charlotte lit it with a candle and carried it with her. Once outside, she was almost overwhelmed by how expansive the darkness was. The deep purple of the sky was salted with stars. The small square of light coming from the cabin was the only sign of habitation for as far as she could see. The immensity of it all was a bit unsettling. The air smelled of damp earth and grass. She led Dusty to the barn to relieve him of the saddle. It was heavy and cumbersome, but she managed to hang it over a wooden sawhorse before dropping it.

Now that Dusty was settled, Charlotte pulled the rifle free from its sheath and carried it back with her to the house. She paused for a moment and looked up at the stars again. It was hard to believe how far she'd come for a dream.

❖

Wes knew Charlotte was right about one thing, she was exhausted. Wes couldn't help wondering what she'd have done if Charlotte hadn't been there. She wasn't sure if she'd have been able to extract the arrow by herself. And then what? The wound would have festered and she'd probably have ended up losing her arm. That's assuming anyone even found her in time.

Living alone on the frontier was challenging under the best circumstances, but throw in illness or injury and you could end up finding yourself in a life-or-death situation. Having help was no guarantee. There was a great deal of luck involved. That was for sure.

She and Clyde had built this homestead together, from nothing. Every time she walked the fields her chest filled with pride at what they'd accomplished so far. Yes, it had been grueling at times, but ultimately, she would gain from whatever effort she put in—and that was rewarding on every level.

She missed Clyde.

Her brother never made her feel that she had to be anyone but herself. She supposed they were both odd in their own ways. Clyde was painfully shy and sensitive. A trait that made him an easy target as a youth amongst his rough-and-tumble clan. He understood on a personal level what it was like to be different so Clyde always gave Wes the space to be different too.

When they'd left the Tennessee hills for the territory, she cut her hair short and began passing as a man. She'd packed only her secondhand shirts and trousers and left her gingham dresses behind. *Good riddance.*

Wes could never have imagined the freedom that a change of clothing would provide. But when she did have time to reflect on it, she realized that personal independence made all the labor of carving a life here worthwhile. Freedom to be exactly who she wanted to be had become her most valued possession. And she wasn't about to risk that on a stranger, regardless of how beguiling Charlotte might be. Or how helpful she'd just been regarding Wes's injured arm. She didn't need a nursemaid or another mouth to feed.

People left comfortable homes to settle in places along the frontier that they knew very little about. But hope was a powerful catalyst, and as Wes had come to realize, external comforts had very little to do with true happiness.

But loneliness was also a powerful force. Wes schooled her emotions as Charlotte crossed the threshold. Charlotte had Wes thinking about things she shouldn't think about, things she'd pretty much given up on. Things like belonging. Things like friendship and affection.

"How is your arm feeling?" Charlotte slid the bar across the door and leaned the rifle in the corner of the main room.

"It hurts." Wes was glad to see that Charlotte had remembered the rifle. In the haze of pain, she'd forgotten to mention it. "But the food was good, thank you." Wes motioned toward the sling with her good arm. "And thank you for this too."

The least she could offer Charlotte was gratitude.

"I'm just glad I was here to help." Charlotte served herself a bowl of food and sat down opposite Wes.

Wes looked away, afraid that if she made eye contact Charlotte would be able to read her thoughts or worse, her emotions. The injury had spooked Wes. She was feeling unsettled and on edge. Now she was going to be laid up for at least a couple of days while her arm mended, maybe longer. She might actually need Charlotte's help for real. That was a frustrating realization.

"I was thinking…"

"Yes?" Charlotte's expression was curious.

"I was thinking that maybe you should stay here for a few days, you know, until you're rested. And until things settle down."

"That's generous of you." Charlotte sampled her food before continuing. "You might need a little help until your arm is better."

It was as if Charlotte *had* read her thoughts, but she wasn't about to admit outright that she needed help.

"Does that hurt?"

Wes's question caught Charlotte by surprise. She looked at Wes, and for a moment wasn't sure what he meant. Then she remembered.

"Oh, that…no, it doesn't hurt." She touched the spot on her temple. It had already started to heal, and besides she had much larger concerns on her mind.

Thinking of her condition when she arrived reminded her that she'd meant to ask Wes something before the whole incident with the arrow.

"I'd like to run a bath if you don't mind." She wanted to wash her hair and remove any remnants from the previous day. "I saw that there is a metal tub at the back of the cabin. I assume that's for laundry and bathing?"

"Yeah. I usually use it outside because it's closer to the well, but I can help you carry it in if you like." Wes sank back in her chair as Charlotte ate. "It's easier to move with two people."

Charlotte was reminded that Wes had recently lost her brother. She still had questions about that, but tonight wasn't the night to ask them.

"Thank you."

"We can bring it in tonight if you like."

"Really? Are you sure you're feeling up to that?" Charlotte worried that Wes needed to lie down and rest after his ordeal.

"I think I can manage."

After she finished eating, the two of them moved the metal basin into the house. They set it down in the bedroom she'd slept in the previous night. Charlotte thought that once Wes was settled into bed, she would draw the quilt and have enough privacy to bathe and wash her hair. The basin was small, barely big enough to sit down in, but if she filled it up enough, then she could use a ladle to douse her hair with water.

Between carrying water from the well and heating it over the fire, it took quite a bit of effort to ready the bath. Wes sat quietly and watched as Charlotte made multiple trips back and forth. By the time the water was deep enough and warm enough to be useful, Wes was ready to turn in.

"Let me help you get a clean shirt on." His damp shirt had mostly dried from sitting by the fire, but it had blood on it and now it also needed to be mended.

"I can do it myself."

He was obviously very shy about taking his shirt off in front of Charlotte. She found his shyness rather endearing.

"Okay." She certainly didn't want to pressure him. "Good night."

"Good night." He shyly tugged the quilt over the door to his bedroom.

CHAPTER THIRTEEN

It took several minutes to get the torn shirt off over the bandage. Wes gently straightened her arm but was careful not to move it too much. There was no way to take the binding off her chest with one hand, so that would just have to keep for another day.

Slowly, she pulled on a clean shirt and then lay on top of the bed, still in her trousers and socks.

Wes tried to relax, but she couldn't find a comfortable position for her injured arm. In the end, she rolled onto her side facing the wall and stabilized her aching arm with her other hand. She could hear Charlotte moving around in the adjacent room. She heard the rustle of clothing being removed and then the light sloshing sound of water.

She closed her eyes and tried not to think about Charlotte. But that was very hard to do. How was it possible that this person she hadn't even known existed a day earlier had now completely invaded her home and her brain?

Charlotte could have easily been killed when the stagecoach was attacked. Wes could have been killed today. Life suddenly seemed so precious and tenuous. Wes took a deep breath and tried to figure out what to do. Charlotte couldn't stay here, that was for sure, but maybe if she stayed a couple of days until Wes's arm was a bit better, then Wes would take Charlotte into Hollister and get her on the next stage heading west. She was sure the Millers who owned the mercantile would put Charlotte up for a few days. Because the longer Charlotte stayed here the more complicated Wes's life would get. Things would be so much easier if her brother was still here. It was interesting to notice that having Charlotte as a house guest had taken her mind off her grief for a little while. Maybe that was a good thing.

❖

The bath, even such a rustic one, was luxurious. Charlotte worked soap through her hair and rinsed it multiple times. She tried her best not to slosh water on the floor, but it was hard to move in such a small tub without getting a little water on the floorboards.

She stepped out of the water and dried off, then wrapped her hair in the towel, twisted the cloth around it, and squeezed to remove as much moisture as possible. Her skin chilled quickly in the cool evening air, despite the warmth of the bath. She slipped a nightgown over her head feeling more refreshed than she'd felt in days. She'd use a bucket to empty the tub tomorrow, but for now, she would just try to relax.

Wes had invited her to stay for a few days, so she had a little more time to be sure of her situation and a little more time to figure out what she could do about it.

Charlotte had worked as a maid at the hotel six days a week, and sometimes seven if they were extra busy. Which was most of the time in the spring when everyone was jumping off to travel west. Everyone called it "jumping off" as if they were setting sail. The prairie schooners did resemble sailing ships with their white canvas covers and wooden buckboards. They'd leave the land-locked port of St. Louis to set sail on the sea of grass that swayed in the breeze like golden waves.

Charlotte had longed for the freedom of leaving. Before Nathaniel, many of her daydreams were filled with thoughts of getting away to somewhere brighter.

Nathaniel had promised her things and she'd stupidly believed him. His eyes had sparkled when he'd talked of traveling west and he'd swept her along with his enthusiasm. And then, like a summer storm, he'd blown away as soon as he'd arrived, leaving destruction in his wake.

In the beginning, she'd been hurt, but now felt herself lucky that she hadn't taken up with a man who would so easily deceive someone he professed to care about. Maybe fate had just dealt her a much better hand.

Still, her options were narrower here. She could either continue traveling west to an unknown future, which would be much more difficult if she was pregnant. That was the first time she'd fully formed her suspicion into a thought, and it was scary. Perhaps she could figure out a way to stay here. It seemed obvious to her that Wes needed someone, even if he didn't quite see it yet himself. Was it possible that fate had brought her to this place for a reason?

Charlotte had been able to come to his rescue with the arrow, but could she really be of help to Wes in a significant way? She knew next to nothing about working a farm or taking care of livestock or frontier cooking, for that matter. Insecurities about her waylaid *grand adventure* swirled in her head keeping her awake.

CHAPTER FOURTEEN

Wes had risen early and gone to check something near the barn when a bout of morning sickness sent Charlotte running for the privy. It seemed that her condition hadn't settled. Her insides were still in revolt. Her sickness, with no other symptoms seemed to confirm her fear. Luckily, Wes hadn't seen her make a run for the door. She was walking back to the cabin when he returned from the barn.

In fact, he wasn't even looking at her at all. He was looking past her. She rotated to see that riders were approaching.

He stepped past her and quickly retrieved the rifle. She wasn't sure how he intended to fire it with one arm. She needn't have worried. He slipped his right arm out of the sling and held the rifle angled at the ground in front of him.

"Maybe you should wait inside." His words were calm, but his body language wasn't.

Charlotte stepped inside and watched from the small window over the sink.

Wes checked to see that Charlotte was inside before turning her attention back to the riders. She stood out front, trying her best to project confidence as the riders approached the cabin. Her arm was aching, but if called upon, she was sure she could still fire the rifle. She counted eight riders, so she would be seriously outmatched. As they drew closer she could see that they were federal soldiers by their blue uniforms, or used to be. The blue of their coats was quite faded from the sun and the whole lot of them had a generally wild and unkept look. She still didn't let her guard down. Out here, soldiers were as unpredictable as drifters.

"Hello. May we approach?" The rider in front called out to her. He raised one hand in a gesture of greeting.

"Sure, I've got no quarrel with you," Wes called out to them. She kept her rifle in a relaxed hold in front of her as they drew closer.

The company of men stopped about twenty feet from the cabin. They were an intimidating, rough looking bunch. They had the look of men who'd been traveling and camping in the open for a while. Their blue jackets were dusty and some of them had scruffy beards.

"We've been dispatched from Fort Scott. I'm Captain Andrews." The man who seemed to be in charge spoke to her. She didn't know much about rank. "We came across a burned-out stage and followed some tracks south."

"Yeah, I did the same yesterday." Wes tried to keep her tone even and non-threatening.

He shifted in his saddle and looked at the man to his left as if they were sharing some private observation.

"Did you come across anyone?" asked the captain.

"No, sir."

"What's your name, son?"

"Wes Holden."

"This your place?"

"Yes."

The captain straightened and his focus shifted. Wes glanced over to see that Charlotte was standing in the doorway. Why had she done that? Wes sidestepped so that she was between Charlotte and the company of men.

"Ma'am." The captain touched his hat. "We'll be on our way. But you and your wife keep an eye out. It would be wise to be on alert until we track down those that attacked the stage."

Wes nodded, keeping direct eye contact with the captain.

She held her stance and watched the riders as they continued south along the trail. She knew the federal troops were supposed to protect homesteaders, but she didn't quite trust them. He'd said they were from Fort Scott, but that was a hundred miles east of where they were. She wasn't sure she believed him. Once they were out of sight, she dropped her injured arm, holding the rifle in one hand.

"Here, let me take that." Charlotte was at her side.

"I told you to stay in the house." Wes didn't release the rifle. Charlotte's hands were on either side of hers as if they were in some sort of standoff.

"I...I thought you might need me."

"A woman has to be careful out here. The rules are different. This isn't St. Louis or Kansas City."

Charlotte couldn't believe Wes was angry, but so was she. All she'd been trying to do was help. And it wasn't as if women had it any better in the city, if the truth were to be told. It was difficult to be a woman alone, period.

"Don't you think I know that?" Charlotte was upset and afraid of a lot more than Wes could possibly know. "Why do you think I left?"

"I don't know—"

"That's right. You don't know." Charlotte took the rifle from him. "You don't know anything about what it's like to be a woman."

She hated that she'd allowed Wes to upset her, but her emotions seemed to be completely beyond her control. Charlotte returned to the cabin with the rifle before she burst into tears. There was nothing more infuriating than tears when you least wanted them.

Wes followed her, but wisely, not too closely.

"I'm sorry." His words had lost the edge they'd had earlier. "I just worry about you is all."

Charlotte couldn't look at him. She busied herself by the cooking pot where she'd made a porridge of oats for breakfast. She sniffed loudly and wiped her cheek with her sleeve.

"Just sit down and eat." She sniffed again.

Wes did as he was told. He quietly waited while she served him a bowl of food and coffee.

"Thank you." He looked down at the steaming bowl rather than at her.

Her Irish side was clearly on display. She'd gotten so angry so fast that she felt a little bad about it. It did seem like Wes was just being protective. Why had that made her so upset?

"I'm sorry too." She cleared her throat as she took the seat opposite him. "I...sometimes my temper gets the better of me."

Charlotte honestly didn't want to fight with the one person who'd shown her kindness in her hour of need. She smiled at Wes, hoping to smooth things over. She'd only taken a few bites when she had a fluttering sensation in her insides, quickly followed by a wave of nausea.

Oh no, first her Irish temper and now this!

She bolted from the chair and ran outside.

Wes was standing in the doorway when she returned.

"You're sick."

"I'm not sick." She couldn't look at him. "Not the way you think."

She worried about being more of a hindrance than a help to Wes. If she was in fact with child that would mean she'd be even more of a burden. Her heart sank. Her options were already limited, and she certainly didn't need more obstacles.

"What does that mean?" He stepped aside to allow her to enter the cabin.

She filled a glass of water from the pitcher near the sink and took a few sips, waiting for her stomach to settle. She knew she wasn't going to be able to hide her condition for much longer.

"I think I might be pregnant."

"Pregnant?" His surprise was obvious. Like it had never even occurred to him.

"Yes."

She slowly rounded the table and took her seat again. She moved the porridge to the side and rested her elbows on the table and her face in her hands.

"How—"

"There was a man in St. Louis...I thought we were to marry." She finally looked at Wes. He quietly waited for her to continue. "He...he left me."

"He left you?"

"At least he also left me with a ticket for the stage. I decided I didn't want to stay in St. Louis. I wanted to build a new life in San Francisco." She took another sip of water. "I had no idea I was pregnant." She paused to allow her statement to sink in. "I can't go back."

Wes stared at her for what seemed like forever.

"Maybe we could help each other." The suggestion seemed to stump Wes. He stared at her and didn't respond so she continued.

"I need someone and you need someone." She was stating the obvious but couldn't help herself. He seemed unaware of the condition he'd been in when she arrived. She knew this was asking a lot and she'd have a lot to learn about homesteading. But she was eager to learn and she was a hard worker. "You can't possibly take care of everything all alone." She paused to let the statement sink in. "Why couldn't we help each other?"

Wes launched to his feet, almost toppling the chair, and crossed the room. He stood holding his injured arm, facing the wall.

"Do you not find me attractive in any way?" Charlotte sensed that Wes was drawn to her, but at the same time afraid of her. He probably had very little experience with women. How could he? She hadn't seen a woman anywhere about since she arrived.

"It's not that." Wes didn't turn to look at her.

"Then what is it?" She got to her feet and stood several feet away from Wes. She wanted to see his face so that she'd have some clue as to what he was thinking. "I know I'm not experienced at farming, but you could show me, and I'm not afraid to work hard."

Wes sensed Charlotte's nearness. She glanced over at Charlotte, who had a curious expression. Charlotte was standing too close so Wes moved as far as she could away from her in the small space.

"It's not what you think." Wes's insides were a churning mess. There was a part of her that wanted to simply blurt it out and tell Charlotte everything. Maybe Charlotte was right. Maybe they could help each other. They were both women alone in the world. But Charlotte didn't really know what she was saying because Wes wasn't the person Charlotte thought she was. Charlotte was only saying these things because she thought Wes was a man.

"Will you explain it to me then?"

"No, I can't."

"Then at least allow me to stay here until the baby comes?" Charlotte's hand rested on her stomach as if for emphasis.

The pregnancy was barely showing so Wes knew that it would be months before the child arrived. She chided herself for not noticing, but in truth she'd gone out of her way not to notice things about Charlotte. There was no way Wes would be able to keep her secret for that long. Charlotte would end up knowing the truth from sheer proximity whether she revealed it or not.

"I don't think I can physically make the trip either back to St. Louis or out west. Please let me stay. I can be of help to you."

"You don't know what you're asking." Wes covered her face with her hand. This wasn't her problem. This was a problem she'd been saddled with because the stage had gotten attacked. But somehow, even in the short time Charlotte had been around Wes had come to realize that she *did* care. She wasn't made of stone, and seeing another woman in a situation not of her own choosing stirred something deep. Wes had to fight the urge to help Charlotte. She needed to look after herself. Didn't she?

As if to echo the raging thoughts in her head, a gust of wind blew the door closed. It banged loudly, causing her to jump. Wes strode to the door and placed the bar over it to keep it still.

"Is there someone else you've made promises too?"

"No, it's not that." Although, maybe she should have lied and said it was. Wes rested her good hand on the door. She faced away from Charlotte.

"Wes, you can trust me." It was as if Charlotte had read her thoughts again.

Could she truly trust Charlotte? Maybe she could.

She rotated slowly and looked at Charlotte for confirmation. Their eyes locked and some small flame lit deep down that warmed Wes's insides. The churning in her head slowed and she remembered the vision she'd had of Charlotte by the hearth. Maybe this was another adventure on which she was meant to embark. Maybe she needed to take a leap of faith. Maybe everything happened for a reason. At personal risk, Charlotte and Wes found themselves together, alone, at the far edge of nowhere. That had to mean something. Charlotte waited for her to respond. The only sound was from the gusting wind outside. Wes lowered her arm. She let it drop loosely at her side, her defenses lowered as she faced Charlotte.

"I'm not Clyde's brother."

"You're not?" Wes's confession clearly surprised Charlotte.

Wes looked at Charlotte and mentally stepped off the cliff.

"I'm his sister."

"Oh." Charlotte blinked rapidly and took a step away from Wes.

For better or worse, Wes told her the truth. Having let go of the lie, Wes felt light as a feather. She was set free. What happened next would be up to Charlotte.

CHAPTER FIFTEEN

Charlotte sat at the table alone with her thoughts. The gusting wind had lessened, and Wes needed to check on the horses and the general condition of things around the farm. Charlotte was grateful for a few minutes to herself to reflect on everything she'd heard.

Charlotte was still coming to terms with the revelation that Wesley Holden was a woman. Despite the way she presented herself to the world, Wes was not a man. This was something that had never occurred to Charlotte as an option. Although now that she knew the truth, some of Wes's behaviors made more sense. Little things she'd noticed about her hands and her face. The level of emotion she allowed Charlotte to witness. Charlotte was surprised that she hadn't figured it out sooner. But why would she have even considered the possibility that Wes was a woman? And if she hadn't figured it out after spending time with Wes for more than twenty-four hours in a small space, then chances were no one else would uncover the truth unless Wes wanted them to. She felt honored on some level that Wes had trusted her enough to be honest.

It was curious to notice that she wasn't particularly bothered by this new information about Wes. Surprised yes, but not upset.

Charlotte was relieved to have a little time to think about this, but nothing she'd discovered changed her mind about wanting to stay. It was almost as if knowing Wes was a woman made her want to stay even more. They truly could support and help each other in ways she hadn't even imagined. It wasn't that she necessarily wanted to be bound to a man in marriage, but she'd thought that was her only option. Wes had shown her another way. A way that might allow both of them to live an independent life on their own terms.

Charlotte reached for her shawl and draped it around her shoulders. The spring air was chilly. The sun had not shown itself all day and was still hidden by clouds. She left the cabin and did her best to avoid puddles as she crossed the mud around the building before reaching the grass. Wes was near the barn with the horses.

When Wes noticed Charlotte, she left the horses and walked in her direction. Wes seemed shy as she approached. Her gaze was downcast and her hand was shoved in her pocket. Wes looked like someone who was afraid she was about to get scolded. But that was literally the last thing on Charlotte's mind.

"How are the horses?"

"Oh, they're fine. I shuffled some dry hay to the top for them." Wes looked over her shoulder in the direction of the barn. And then back at Charlotte. "How are you?"

Charlotte appreciated the warmth in Wes's question. It was as if sharing their truths had lowered some barrier that had existed between them. Wes was definitely less defensive, even her stance was more open.

"I'm okay. How are you?"

Wes shrugged with a half-smile.

"What?"

"Well, I sort of expected you to run for the hills, but here you are." Wes scuffed at the ground with the toe of her boot.

"There literally aren't any hills to run to." Charlotte smiled at her own joke.

"I suppose that's true." Wes smiled back.

"I wondered if you could show me around the property a little?" Charlotte had arrived in sort of a bad way and then the storm had kept them indoors. She hadn't really gotten a tour of the homestead.

"Sure." Wes looked down at Charlotte's skirt already soaking up water from the wet grass. "As long as you don't mind getting your feet wet. The grass is pretty high."

"I'll be alright."

Wes started walking toward the back of the cabin. There was a large plowed field between the cabin and the tree line.

"Where you see the trees, that's the creek." Wes extended her arm in a sweeping motion. "The boundary of the claim follows the creek south. You can see the lower field in the distance. That's corn and potatoes." Wes rotated and pointed north. "The upper field is also corn with some beans and carrots along the edge. The northern boundary basically sits right on the horizon you see from here."

"How many acres in all?"

"One hundred and sixty." Wes rested her hand on her hip and surveyed the plowed field. "Since there were two of us we were able to double the acreage." Wes met Charlotte's gaze. "It was our dream. And someday we thought we'd even have some cattle to graze here."

There were long swaths of water between the raised rows of green sprigs. The water reflected the clouds above as if the ground was transparent in the narrow puddles and you were looking at something from beneath rather than above. The air was heavy with the scent of dampness.

When she glanced back, Wes seemed sad all of a sudden.

"Clyde is buried over there under that cottonwood."

"Do you mind if we walk to his grave?" She hadn't even thought to ask before now and considered maybe it would do Wes some good. Grieving was different for everyone and couldn't be rushed. Wes was still in the midst of it. Charlotte knew that ignoring it or not talking about it certainly didn't help.

Wes nodded and then started walking in that direction. Charlotte tried to keep up, but the heels of her shoes kept sinking into the soft, wet ground. At one point she thought she might lose her shoe completely until Wes circled back to assist. She offered Charlotte her hand and then bent down to free her foot from the mud. Wes's hand was warm and strong, and Charlotte wouldn't have minded holding it for longer. But Wes released her as soon as they began walking again. If there was any friendly comfort in their brief contact it seemed that Charlotte was the only one who'd noticed it or welcomed it.

The grave was nothing more than a mound of dark earth surrounded by prairie grass. There was no marker. But the nearby tree would be a sentinel and the sound of the creek was pleasing. This was as good a place as any to rest.

Wes stood quietly and watched Charlotte as she took everything in. Charlotte stared at the grave for a long time and then up at the tree, then she closed her eyes as if she were meditating on something. It was strange to stand at the graveside with someone else. Until today there'd been no other mourners except herself. It was strange to think that someone's whole existence could just cease to be. And that was it—nothingness. All that you hoped for, all that you felt, buried in the ground. Dust to dust, as the Good Book said.

She'd lost herself in thought and didn't realize Charlotte was studying her until she spoke.

"I still think we could help one another." Charlotte held her shawl with one hand and brushed a loose strand of hair from her face with the other.

"What do you mean?" Wes didn't see how Charlotte could help her but was willing to listen.

"We are both women who were willing to venture far to live an independent life. We could still do that. We could work together for that common goal."

"I don't want to live the way I used to." Wes wasn't going back to her old habit of dressing. She was used to making her own way now and wouldn't settle for less.

"I don't want my former life either." Charlotte paused as if she was having a hard time finding the right words for something. She looked toward the creek and then back at Wes. "I could stay here with you, and you could be who you are now. I don't want you to change…no one would have to know but us."

"Are you saying—?"

"We could marry and work this place together. I meant it when I said you need help. You can't do everything by yourself and I can't either. And I certainly can't go back to St. Louis, not like this. We could help each other, Wes."

"How can we get married?" The very thought of it upended Wes's stomach. It was one thing to live as a man; it seemed like quite another thing to involve a whole other person in the charade.

"As far as what people see, you are a man and I am a woman." Charlotte's unwavering gaze almost made Wes believe it could work. "I was romanced, then abandoned and now I'm almost certainly pregnant. I *can't* go back to the life I had before. You are a woman who has taken on the life of a man to fulfill a dream of independence. Working together, we can protect each other's secrets and have the life we both want."

"Working a farm like this, building it from nothing, isn't easy." Was she actually considering what Charlotte was proposing? Maybe she was. Could this be the glimmer of light at the end of a very long, dark tunnel?

"I'm not afraid of hard work." Charlotte seemed determined.

"Are you sure about this?"

"I think I am." Charlotte smiled. "But if you want to sleep on it, I understand."

Wes nodded and looked at the ground as they walked back across the field. She wasn't sure what to say or even if this entire idea was too good to be true. Could she trust Charlotte? An outsider and someone she'd barely just met?

Wes needed time to think. She'd lingered at the creek with the excuse of clearing storm debris and sent Charlotte back to the house. But the truth was she needed a little space.

The sun was dropping below the horizon. The last threads of daylight remained, drawing her attention to the sunset. Maybe God did care after all. Maybe God hadn't forsaken her, despite her lack of attention to matters of the church. Charlotte had arrived just when Wes needed her most. That had to mean something. Charlotte's suggestion that they help each other was settling into a comfortable spot inside her head. Out here on the edge of the world, who would know besides the two of them?

Chapter Sixteen

Charlotte sat nearby as Wes added wood to the fire, just enough to warmly light the room. It was nice to have a little time to study Wes without her really noticing. Now that she knew that Wes was a woman, it was still hard to get her mind to accept it. Wes had either practiced masculine behavior or it came to her naturally. She seemed very comfortable in trousers and a collared shirt. Of course, it wasn't only the clothing, Wes's gestures and general movements were those of a boy for sure. She marveled how at ease Wes seemed now. The previous day Wes had been unable to even look at her, much less casually stoke the fire while Charlotte looked on.

"How many people know?"

"Know what?" Wes sat down and adjusted her arm in the sling.

"That you're a woman." Charlotte was curious.

"Clyde knew. And now you know."

Charlotte was quiet for a moment. She wondered what it felt like to carry a secret so big.

"No one else knows?" That was hard to believe, but it must be the case.

"There are no neighbors close, except the Caufields. And there was no need to tell anyone." Wes shifted in her chair. "People see what they want to see."

"That's true." Charlotte knew that to be a fact. People in the city looked past the hardship. They would literally pass someone by without really seeing them. Working as a maid meant Charlotte felt practically invisible also.

"What about you?"

"What about me?" Charlotte looked over at Wes.

"Who was your fellow?"

"Nathaniel Finch." Simply saying his name brought back the anger and hurt.

"You really loved him?"

"I thought I did." Charlotte cocked her head to one side and sighed. "I think I was probably more in love with the *idea* of him, than who he actually was. I was foolish."

Wes had noticed the way Charlotte bit her bottom lip when she was thinking. She was doing it now.

"I was naive. I shouldn't have trusted him. I was so stupid."

It bothered Wes that someone would take advantage of Charlotte. For some reason, Charlotte brought out all Wes's protective tendencies. She wanted nothing more than to keep Charlotte safe.

"You weren't stupid to trust someone that you thought cared about you."

"I don't know…" Charlotte's words trailed off. "In hindsight, I should have known better. I should have seen him for who he was."

She was quiet for a long moment. "I suppose I was desperate to believe in him. Even though I worked almost every day I was barely scraping by in the city." She turned away from the glow of the fire and looked at Wes with a wistful expression. "Truthfully, I'd rather scrape by here where you literally reap what you sow, than go back to my life in the city."

Without full legal standing, most single women could not escape the confines of poverty by themselves. As a pioneering family, they would be a unit. A self-contained unit for survival. As a result, women on the frontier found themselves on a far more equal footing with their spouses. But Charlotte would have a lot to learn, and Wes knew she'd be the one who'd have to teach her.

They were quiet for a little while. The whole situation seemed surreal to Wes. Three days ago, she'd been desperately lonely and grieving the loss of her only family. And now she was sitting by the fire talking to a woman who had suggested they marry. It was almost too much to consider.

She thought of the arrow through her arm, of the burned-out stagecoach, and the soldiers who'd paid them a visit. Wes needed to help Charlotte learn how to defend herself if she was going to stay this far from more settled places.

"Tomorrow, I should show you how to use the rifle."

Charlotte regarded her with wide eyes.

"In case anything ever happened when I wasn't around." Wes didn't want to scare Charlotte, but she didn't want Charlotte to be left unprotected either.

"Okay." Charlotte nodded. "Thank you."

CHAPTER SEVENTEEN

Wes came in from the field to find Charlotte mending her shirt. Her jacket hung on a nearby chair having already been repaired. Two days had passed since Charlotte introduced the idea that they could live together and work the farm. Wes had to admit that it had been nice to return after hours of labor to find that there was hot food to eat. Not only that, the cabin had never looked so good. It seemed that neither she nor her brother were very good housekeepers. Wes hadn't realized that until she witnessed the difference Charlotte made. It was the little things, clean dishes, clean pots, laundry boiled properly over the fire pit and then hung to dry in a way that didn't make shirts look as if they'd been wadded up for days.

Charlotte was obviously making the case for why she should stay. Wes still wasn't sure it would work and she didn't want to be forced into something she hadn't had time to completely think through.

"You don't have to do that." Wes took her hat off and hung it by the door.

"I had a sewing kit and I didn't mind the distraction while I waited for the cornbread to bake." Charlotte held the shirt at arm's length to examine her handiwork. "I'm sorry the thread color doesn't quite match the shirt."

At one time, the shirt had been white, but years of wear and poor laundry skills had turned it to a mottled gray color. Charlotte's white stitches could be seen just below the shoulder and across the hole where the arrow had pierced her arm.

"How is your shoulder feeling?" Charlotte had obviously seen her rub her arm, just below the wound. She studied Wes from her seat at the table.

"It's alright." Wes lied. It hurt like hell, and she hadn't been able to get as much done since her injury. She'd barely used her injured arm, but it still ached. She tried to keep it in the sling, but sometimes needed her other hand to steady herself or grasp something.

"I should probably change the bandage." Charlotte stood and set the mended shirt aside with the jacket. "Why don't you sit down and I'll take a look."

First, there was dinner already in the works, and her shirt mended, and now Charlotte was going to fuss over her injured arm. She wasn't sure how much kindness she could tolerate. Charlotte was definitely wearing her down, despite her best efforts to maintain a cordial distance while she tried to sort out what to do.

Wes reluctantly sat down. She was too beat to argue, and Charlotte was probably right about changing the bandage, which Wes couldn't easily do herself.

"Do you want to take your arm out of the sleeve so that I can get a better look?"

Now that Charlotte knew the truth it wasn't such a big deal to take off her shirt, but Wes wasn't the sort of person who ever enjoyed parading around in her birthday suit. She'd been shy as a youngster, probably because she was self-conscious about her body, which never blossomed in the way other girls' bodies seemed to do. As an adult, she was probably still shier than most. But in this instance, modesty would only hinder a task that needed doing. She unbuttoned her shirt and gingerly slid her right arm free of the sleeve. She still had a sleeveless undershirt on anyway.

Charlotte leaned closer to take a look. Blood had soaked through the bandage on one side and dried to a dark brown color. Charlotte slowly unwound the cloth and then lightly touched the area around where they'd cauterized the wound.

"Is this tender?"

"A little." Wes tried to see the spot but couldn't.

"It's a little red, but I don't think it's infected." Charlotte straightened with her hands on her hips. "It was a good idea to cauterize it, I think."

Charlotte filled a basin with water and pulled a chair close so that she could clean the area where the bandage had been. She was too close for Wes's liking. Wes could smell her hair and some other scent, a mixture of lavender and rose water. When Charlotte leaned closer to examine the injury more carefully, Wes could feel the soft caress of Charlotte's breath on her skin. The sensation sent a chill down her arm and she had to look away.

"After it dries, I can dress it again with a fresh bandage." Charlotte set the basin aside. "We could eat and then I can take care of this after dinner."

"Thank you." Wes nodded. She was feeling fairly hungry. And the cornbread was smelling pretty good.

Charlotte studied Wes from the fireside as she cut slices of the hot cornbread from the pan. She worried that Wes was trying to do too much with her injured arm. Regardless of how much she tried to help out around the place Wes wouldn't take time off from her chores. They also hadn't yet discussed the plan she'd suggested. Two days had passed, and Charlotte was afraid that Wes might still decide to ask her to leave.

Bouts of morning sickness earlier in the day had made her feel even more unsettled. She was in a near panic, feeling completely out of options, but trying not to reveal her desperation to Wes so as not to appear too needy. She wanted to prove more than anything that she could be an asset to Wes, without coming right out and saying it. Although, she didn't think she'd be able to keep quiet forever.

As long as she kept busy with tasks, she could function. But at night, left alone with her thoughts, her mind spiraled to dark places of fear. She was angry at Nathaniel for leaving her in this situation; she was possibly even angrier at herself for allowing it to happen. He'd been insistent, yes, and persistent, annoyingly so, but in the end, she had no one to blame but herself. If the world was a hard place for a single woman to survive, being a single woman with a child was exponentially more difficult, if not impossible.

Charlotte set a plate of cornbread and beans in front of Wes.

"Thank you." Wes looked at Charlotte with an expression that was hard to decipher. "Is everything okay?"

Wes must have sensed her worry. What could she possibly say? Should she just be honest?

"It's nothing." She tried to smile but felt insincere about it. She wasn't really happy.

"Are you sure?"

Charlotte sat across from Wes. After a moment, she looked up and met Wes's gaze.

"Honestly, I think I'm just a little tired." She considered asking again but had second thoughts. She'd been the one to bring it up the first time. She'd feel a lot more stable if Wes actually broached the subject the next time they spoke about it.

"You should eat something."

Wes had obviously noticed that she was merely moving food around on her plate. Worry was robbing her of an appetite, that and the morning sickness.

"You're right." She smiled weakly and then took a few bites of cornbread. She feared that Wes considered her more of a burden than an asset. And if pressed, how could she argue. Making a decent skillet of cornbread wasn't enough. Charlotte felt the need to prove to Wes that she could help in some other important way. She just didn't know exactly what way that was.

Chapter Eighteen

Wes decided the next morning to go hunting. The fields were in good shape at the moment and Wes was needing a little time to herself. The supply of cured venison was dwindling, and whether Charlotte stayed or not more would be needed.

"I was thinking I'd go out today and hunt."

Charlotte poured the last of the coffee into Wes's cup.

"Oh." Charlotte set the pot on the table and took her seat. "How long will you be gone?"

Wes shrugged. "As long as it takes."

She hadn't meant the statement to sound quite as callous as it came out.

"Sometimes it can take all day." She met Charlotte's gaze over the top of her coffee cup.

"I see."

It was hard to know what Charlotte was thinking. She fussed with the front of her dress and wouldn't look up at Wes again. Was she upset? Well, that wasn't Wes's problem. They needed meat and hunting was the only way to get it. She didn't want to kill any of the chickens if she could avoid it. Not as long as they were still laying eggs.

"Bar the door while you're inside." Wes wondered if Charlotte was still feeling uneasy after what had happened to the stagecoach.

Charlotte nodded but still didn't look up. If she wanted to say more, she didn't. After a moment, Charlotte got up and began to clear the table. Wes sensed that Charlotte was upset about something, but she honestly didn't want to talk about anything this morning. Having a nearly total stranger in her small cabin was beginning to cause her anxiety. She didn't want to hurt Charlotte's feelings, but she most certainly would if she didn't get out and clear her head.

"I'm sure I won't be gone too long." Wes downed the last swallow of coffee, then reached for her hat and then the rifle.

"Be careful." Charlotte seemed sincere.

Wes was reminded that the last time she left Charlotte alone she came back with an arrow sticking out of her arm. Now she felt a little bad about being so abrupt.

"What happened last time…that was a rare thing."

Charlotte nodded.

"And anyway, I'll be careful." Wes smiled as she stepped through the door.

Her arm was feeling better. Wes left the sling behind. She saddled Dusty, careful not to overreach with her still healing arm. She slid the rifle into its sheath, and then nudged Dusty north along the creek. She'd look for deer tracks in the soft mud along the creek bed.

After she'd been riding for a little while, she rotated in the saddle to check the distance from the cabin which was now nothing more than a small square on the horizon.

In the beginning, isolation was forced upon her and she'd accepted it as an inevitable outcome of staking a claim at the edge of an unsettled world. And then even more so after the loss of her brother. But after a few days in close proximity to someone else, she realized that she'd actually come to enjoy solitude.

Solitude had its own rewards which could only be known to a person in quiet moments. Neighbors on the frontier lived so far apart that they rarely saw more than the blue smoke of each other's chimneys in the distance. The openness of the prairie on every side provided room to breathe, to expand, and to wander. Room for the unhampered discovery of self.

Most folks must have similar longings, although Wes had never spoken of such things to anyone, not even her brother. But he must have felt it too.

The life she had built here would sustain her. She had freedom and air and elbow room. Wes was liberated and beholden to no one. But where did that leave Charlotte?

Wes spotted a downed tree in the shade near the creek and decided to sit for a spell. She tied Dusty to the low-hanging branch of a willow tree so that he could nibble grass in the shade. Wes propped the rifle next to where she sat on the ground, leaning her back against the fallen tree trunk. The tree had been on the ground for a long time, the bark had been chewed or weathered off in a large swath exposing the soft wood underneath.

She propped her forearms on her knees, allowing her hands to droop and relax. The sound of the stream was soothing. Bird calls were the only other sound nearby.

Wes closed her eyes and thought back to her brief layover in St. Louis. It was not a place she could have stayed for long. Too many people all in competition for survival, most of them focused solely on making money off travelers or the business of westward expansion.

She thought of Charlotte in that place, with a baby. It didn't take much effort to imagine how scared Charlotte must be feeling about her prospects.

Solitude was appealing, but was that the long-term vision she'd had for her life? Wes had thought from time to time that she might eventually marry, although for her, a traditional marriage seemed more complicated. So she had resigned herself to the notion that it might never happen. Was that partly why solitude appealed to her? Because the alternative seemed worse? Finding herself locked into a traditional marriage to a man seemed a worse fate than living alone.

But Charlotte had presented her with an idea she'd never even considered. To join with a woman, a friend. To join with someone for mutual support and comfort and maybe even affection. That last thought had only recently come to her. Even the lightest, briefest touch from Charlotte made her feel less lonely. Charlotte made her feel seen for who she truly was.

Charlotte was right in thinking she couldn't go back to St. Louis, and traveling on seemed fraught with peril.

Wouldn't having a wife and child only serve to further shore up her disguise? Wes would be above reproach as a man.

Pragmatically, the arrangement made sense. But they hardly knew each other. Was it too soon to join up with someone Wes had only just met?

Having abandoned the pretense of hunting entirely, Wes relaxed and allowed the sound of the babbling stream to slow her racing thoughts.

❖

Charlotte stepped out of the dark interior of the cabin into the sunlight. She stood for a moment, hands on hips, and surveyed the farm. She had been trying to temper her excitement about the possibility of staying on. Wes certainly hadn't said yes, and Charlotte was trying not to get her hopes up. But it was hard not to imagine the joyfulness of a child running about the place. What an amazing setting this would be to grow up in.

The fields were lined with sprigs of green as if someone had painted long lines with chartreuse paint on top of the dark, tilled earth. Charlotte didn't know anything about farming really, but from the size of the fields it seemed impossible that Wes would be able to harvest everything by herself. Charlotte wasn't an expert on getting things to grow, certainly, but she could surely pick corn or dig potatoes once they were ready. If allowed to remain, she would show Wes that her ability to help with the harvest had value. She was not above any menial task that needed doing.

Some wildflowers had sprouted at the end of one of the rows and she bent to pick them, thinking they might brighten up the table for supper. Charlotte was skilled at finding pleasure in the small things.

Ned was grazing not too far from the barn so she sauntered in his direction. He raised up when she drew closer, and she spoke softly to him as she rubbed his velvet nose.

"Hi there, boy. How is your day going?"

Something in the nearby grass caught her eye. For a second, she thought it was a stick, but then it moved and she realized it was a snake. She froze. The snake slid casually closer, its tongue slithering in and out to test the air. What should she do? Run or stay still? Charlotte couldn't remember. The snake moved within a few feet of where she stood and then stopped. She watched, almost mesmerized, as the snake began to slowly wrap itself into a coil. Charlotte tried to remain as calm as possible, not making any sudden moves, as she filled her fingers with Ned's mane and urged him to move away from the snake. When she heard the unmistakable rattle of its tail, she ran, and luckily, Ned followed.

Charlotte was breathless when she reached the edge of the yard, nearest the cabin. She looked back, half expecting the snake to follow but of course it hadn't.

"What's the matter?"

Charlotte half jumped out of her skin at the sound of Wes's voice. Wes had come from behind the house, leading Dusty by the reins. Charlotte hadn't seen Wes approach. She definitely had to learn to be more aware of her surroundings in general.

"A rattlesnake…over there." She pointed to the grassy area on the south side of the barn.

"Show me." Wes slid the rifle out of the leather sheath.

Charlotte tried her best to remember the exact spot. She approached the general area with great caution. Wes stayed close, right at her elbow. After a minute of searching the tall grass where she'd been petting Ned, she saw the snake.

"There." She put her hand on Wes's arm.

"Okay, step back."

"Are you going to shoot it?" That seemed like a ridiculous question the moment she uttered it.

"Snakes don't bother me, but a rattlesnake this close to the barn and the house does."

"Be careful, Wes."

Wes looked over at Charlotte. There was genuine concern in her expression. Charlotte was a sweet woman.

"I'll be careful." Wes smiled at her.

Less than ten feet away, a five-foot rattlesnake lay fully extended in the afternoon sun. It had obviously fed on a field mouse or something recently because a lump distorted its middle.

Wes took aim at the snake's head and pulled the trigger. She got him on the first shot. She strode to the serpent, reached down, and held it up by the tail which had at least eight rattlers. She rotated to show Charlotte, but Charlotte slunk back as if she'd seen a horrible monster or as if she might pass out. One slender hand rested across her chest, the other covered her mouth.

"Don't worry. He's good and dead." Wes glanced back at the snake carcass dangling from her hand. "Do you want to keep the rattlers as a souvenir?"

The question hardly crossed her lips when she saw Charlotte sway on her feet and then crumple to the ground. In a flash, Wes dropped the snake and rushed to Charlotte's side. She laid the rifle on the ground and gently slipped her arm under Charlotte's shoulder and cradled Charlotte in her lap. This was the second time Charlotte had ended up in her arms. Once during their first meeting and now again.

Wes held Charlotte against her chest. Charlotte's head lolled to one side. Wes brushed her fingertips across Charlotte's cheek. After a few seconds, Charlotte's lashes fluttered. She looked up at Wes, and in that moment all Wes could think of was that she wanted to lose herself in the pools of Charlotte's green eyes. A wave of protectiveness crashed over her. In that moment, she wanted nothing more than to keep Charlotte from harm. She rocked back on her heels but didn't release Charlotte and Charlotte didn't ask to be let go.

CHAPTER NINETEEN

Charlotte watched Wes clean the rifle before placing it in the corner of the small living space. They'd eaten dinner in almost complete silence. It seemed that Wes was working something out and Charlotte hadn't wanted to press her. Wes had come back from the hunting excursion empty-handed, so perhaps she was frustrated about that. Charlotte was still a little embarrassed that she'd fainted at the sight of the dead snake. Wes must think of her as such a fragile woman, far too weak to survive as a frontier wife. Charlotte was disappointed with herself. But in her defense, the pregnancy seemed to be wreaking havoc on her emotions and the stability of her stomach. She was on the verge of throwing up one moment and bursting into tears the next.

"I've been thinking."

Wes's statement came out of nowhere. Charlotte jumped and then was annoyed at herself for being so on edge. *Get hold of yourself, woman.*

"Sorry, I didn't mean to startle you." Wes rested her elbows on the edge of the table and studied Charlotte.

"It's not you, I'm just…unsettled." Charlotte left the fireside and took a seat across from Wes. "You said you've been thinking about something?"

Charlotte was afraid of what Wes was about to say, but she tried to hide that fact from Wes. Her hand began to tremble, and she dropped it to her lap out of view.

"I've been thinking that maybe you're right."

Charlotte held her breath, waiting for Wes to continue.

"I think maybe we could help each other."

"You mean that?" Relief tingled along Charlotte's frayed nerves. She didn't want to get ahead of herself, but it was hard not to.

"I don't want you to leave." Wes rubbed her hands together. She focused on her hands rather than Charlotte. Finally, she looked up at Charlotte. "I would worry about you...and the baby."

"Oh, Wes, you won't be sorry." She reached across the table and covered Wes's hands with hers. "I promise to be a help to you. And I'm sure once the pregnancy is further along I'll feel better."

"I'm guessing you don't really like snakes." The corner of Wes's mouth quirked up in a half smile.

Charlotte laughed. She noticed that Wes hadn't pulled away when she'd touched her hands. And in fact, Wes was holding her hands too. Charlotte's heart thumped in her chest. This was what she'd wished for and she hadn't even known it existed. A place to call home. A safe haven in a harsh world. Wes would take care of her and she would take care of Wes.

"Partners?" She squeezed Wes's hands lightly.

Wes smiled.

"Partners."

Charlotte could hardly contain herself. The thought of leaving and being on her own, pregnant was keeping her up at night. She couldn't imagine how it would feel to leave that worry behind and know that she and Wes would be there for each other.

"We should probably take a trip into Hollister in a few days and see if we can find the circuit preacher." Wes had obviously taken her proposition very seriously.

"You mean—?" Charlotte didn't want to assume.

"Well, I don't think it would look right for you to be here and be with child if folks thought we were unmarried." Wes took a breath and sat back in her chair. "That's if I am to continue to live as a man."

"Right. I agree." Charlotte had suggested the idea herself and it seemed the most prudent.

"It's a little strange to think that we could get married, but I'm all for making things official so that you and the baby are protected."

Charlotte's chest grew warm with affection for Wes. Here was a woman who hardly knew Charlotte but was willing to throw her life in with Charlotte's for Charlotte's sake. No one had ever done such a kindness for her before, and she wouldn't forget this.

"Thank you." Those two simple words seemed completely inadequate for the immense gratitude Charlotte was feeling. "You are doing me a great kindness, Wes."

"As I see it, we're doing it for each other." Wes paused. "I'm honestly not sure I could manage here alone. It will require hard work from both of us, but you'll have a home for as long as you want it."

Wes looked away, her voice choked by emotion. And Charlotte wondered if Wes was thinking of her brother. Wes had suffered a loss and was surely still dealing with that. Charlotte got up from her chair and rounded the table. She put her arms around Wes's shoulders from behind and hugged her. Wes curled her fingers around Charlotte's wrist and squeezed lightly as if to return some small measure of affection.

Wes struck Charlotte as someone who hadn't allowed herself to show emotion, let alone affection. Charlotte hoped that in some small way, her friendship could ease some of Wes's burden.

❖

Wes undressed slowly at the bedside. She'd sat up for a while by the dying fire, lost in thought. She slid her injured arm out of the shirtsleeve and flexed her bicep. The injury still ached, but it showed no sign of infection. She tugged on a nightshirt and reclined on the bed as quietly as she could manage. The bedframe still creaked when she lay down with her full weight.

She was lying on her back, looking up at the rafters, reflecting on the day. She sort of couldn't believe she had suggested they actually go through with Charlotte's plan. They were going to get married, in front of God and everyone. There would be no going back to the person she'd been in Tennessee. Not that she ever for one minute thought about doing that, but this sort of decision did add a level of finality to the path she'd chosen. Because now it wasn't just herself, but her decisions would also affect another person.

Responsibility for someone else had a certain weight to it. Wes was trying that on for size, deciding whether she liked the fit of it. She had to admit that it felt good. The notion that someone needed her was a sobering thought and at the same time affirming.

She thought of her brother and how his life had been cut short. He never got the chance to have a wife or children and now Wes was about to have both. Life was so strange. Things happened or they didn't, things worked out or they didn't, and most times you had no control over any of it.

Wes rolled onto her side, onto her good arm, and pulled the blanket up over her shoulder.

Everything in her life was about to change. She knew that but didn't really know exactly how. The whole notion of marriage, of living with someone full time, probably should have made her as nervous as a long-tailed cat in a room full of rocking chairs. But instead she was at peace with her decision. If asked she'd have simply said, it just feels right. It had been a long time since she'd felt so sure of anything.

CHAPTER TWENTY

Charlotte set her bag, some blankets, and a lunch basket in the back of the buckboard. Ned and Dusty grazed nearby, not yet hitched to the wagon. The spring rains had cleared, and Wes thought the road might be in good enough condition to make the trip to Hollister. They'd spent a week together and had settled into a friendly rhythm of cohabitation. That week further convinced Charlotte that her plan could work. Charlotte smiled, thinking of how much had changed in a week. She was safe and she had Wes to thank for sheltering her. As far as anyone else was concerned, she would be a married woman before the baby really started to show.

Wes was out checking some things around the farm before they were going to leave because they expected the trip to take at least two days, maybe three. If the circuit preacher wasn't in Hollister, then they'd have to travel as far as Emporia to get legally married. Maybe that would be even better. Wes didn't know anyone in Emporia and neither did she.

Movement caught her attention. A rider was approaching. Should she get the rifle? Should she call for Wes? She scanned the homestead but didn't see Wes. She was likely out in the field, far from view. Before fear could fully set in, the rider waved.

"Hello there." His greeting was friendly.

"Hello." She stood with the wagon between them as he drew closer.

"I'm Ben Caufield." He didn't dismount. He was holding something in one hand that was covered with a cloth. He had a gentle manner about him and a kind face well-tanned by the sun. "My wife Maddie and I have the place just south of here."

"It's nice to meet you." She remembered now that Wes had talked about the Caufields. She allowed her nerves to calm. "I'm Charlotte."

"Is Wes around?" Ben seemed surprised to see her. And unsure of what to do next.

"I'm guessing he's out in the field. Shall I fetch him?" Charlotte was careful to use the right pronouns, even though now she knew the truth.

"No need." Ben held the dish out to her. "My wife sent this for Wes. It's a sweet potato pie."

"Thank you so much." Charlotte accepted the gift. "I'll be sure and let Wes know you came by."

"I'll let Maddie know there's a woman on the place. She'll be so happy to hear that Wes isn't alone." He seemed momentarily embarrassed that he'd said too much. He cleared his throat. "She'll be happy to have another woman nearby."

"I would be very pleased to meet her." Charlotte held the pie with both hands. It smelled delicious. "I just recently arrived by stage from St. Louis." She felt like she needed to reveal some small detail of how she came to be there.

"Oh, I suppose you met Wes when he and Clyde worked in St. Louis?" He seemed pleased that he was putting this puzzle together.

"Yes." She figured a white lie wouldn't hurt. She had no idea Wes had worked in St. Louis, but that seemed like a very plausible detail to exploit when explaining why she was here and how they'd met.

"Well, tell Wes I came by." He touched the brim of his hat and smiled as he turned back toward the path south.

Charlotte added the home baked pie to the rest of the food she'd packed in the basket. Wes rounded the cabin just as Ben was about to disappear from view.

"Was that Ben?" Wes joined Charlotte.

"Yes, his wife sent you a pie."

"I'll bet he was surprised to see you." Wes arched her eyebrows and the side of her mouth curled up in a half smile.

"He asked if we met when you worked in St. Louis. I hope it was okay that I said we did."

"That's as good a story as any." Wes shrugged. "Although, it'll probably still come out that you were on the stage that got held up."

Wes hitched the horses to the wagon as she talked. Her movements were confident and methodical. Charlotte realized that Wes had lots of innate knowledge about how to do things, like tend crops and horses and how to hunt and dry meat. Things Charlotte had never learned. Her respect for Wes grew with each day that passed. She looked forward to learning from Wes about how to be more self-sufficient.

"Luckily, one story only serves to support the other."

Wes nodded as she held out her hand to assist Charlotte onto the high front seat of the wagon.

"Thank you." She looked down at Wes and smiled. Wes didn't have to defer to her the way that she did. They were both women. But it seemed to be in Wes's nature to assume all the manners of a man. Charlotte didn't mind. She felt cared for when Wes fussed over her.

"Let me just get the rifle and we'll be on our way."

Wes disappeared into the cabin and returned with her coat in one hand and the rifle in the other. She set both in the bed of the wagon and then hoisted herself up beside Charlotte.

The wagon swayed like a boat as they traversed the rough path north toward the main road. With each lurch of the seat, Charlotte found herself pressed against Wes's shoulder and arm. Luckily, it was her right arm. Wes's injured left arm was much better, but still she'd have worried if she'd been continually bumping it. Wes held the reins loosely in both hands, at ease holding the two-horse team.

"I didn't realize you'd ever been to St. Louis." Charlotte was a little surprised that Wes hadn't mentioned it.

"Clyde and I worked the docks there for a few months to make money for our kit."

Charlotte tried to imagine running into Wes in a different environment. Would she have noticed Wes? Probably. Wes was quite good-looking. Those intense, dark eyes would definitely have caught her attention if they'd met on the street.

"I didn't much care for the city. I can see why you wanted to leave." Wes turned to look at her. "Too many people, plus the smells."

"Yes, that's one thing I don't miss for sure. The air here smells so good."

They were quiet for a few minutes, then Wes continued, as if she'd just remembered the rest of the story.

"Even with what we'd saved it was still rough going for the first year." Wes stared at the horizon as if she were seeing the past out there somewhere. "We roofed the cabin with a frame of rafters and roughly hewn bark shingles. But for the first year, all we had was a dirt floor. It took another year to put the wooden flooring in." Wes paused. "Someday I'd like to have real glass in the windows."

"It's hard to imagine building a house from the ground up. Really, doing everything all by yourselves." Charlotte imagined that the spot where the cabin sat had once been undisturbed grassland similar to what surrounded them now in every direction.

It was daunting to consider that their very survival depended on their ability to grow, harvest, hunt, and store almost everything they would need to get them through the winter. Some supplies were available in Hollister, like flour and sugar and coffee. You could buy bolts of cloth for dresses if you had money or something else to barter, but most everything had to be made or grown by hand.

They stopped along the way for lunch and then traveled another hour before reaching Hollister. It was interesting for Charlotte to make the trip back toward Hollister since the first time she had paid very little attention to anything outside the coach. Then she'd walked in a daze from the Santa Fe Trail to Wes's cabin. Charlotte felt as if she was truly seeing the landscape now. As if she were seeing it for the first time.

The ride had been mostly grassland. They hadn't passed any other houses until they got to Hollister which, as far as towns went, was pretty small. The *town* only had a mercantile, a small boarding house, and a restaurant. There was a livery where she remembered that the coach had stopped briefly for fresh horses.

Wes brought Ned and Dusty to a stop at the side of the mercantile. It was a wood-framed structure with a tall facade but otherwise a very simple square building. The siding had seen some weather. The whitewash had faded to gray in several places. There were two large windows on either side of the front door.

Wes jumped down and tied the horses to a post before rounding the wagon to help her climb down. It wasn't that she wasn't agile enough to dismount without assistance, but everything was a bit more complicated in a long skirt and petticoat. Having spent a week working on the farm, she could definitely see the advantage to trousers, although she wasn't interested in abandoning her dresses anytime soon, if ever. Hopefully, the new life she'd chosen wouldn't require her to do so.

"I'd like to introduce you to Wade and Martha Miller. They own this place." Wes held her hand longer than necessary after helping Charlotte down from the seat. Wes seemed to realize she was still holding Charlotte's hand and quickly released it. "Um, they'll know if the circuit preacher is around."

"I'm happy to rest for a moment." The hard seat and the bumpy ride made her lower back ache a little.

They climbed the steps to the front porch and Wes held the door for Charlotte to enter. The low hum of voices greeted them. The store wasn't packed, but there were a few men talking with a man behind the counter who she assumed was the owner, Wade. And a woman and child milled around near bolts of cloth spread out on a table at the back.

"Wes Holden. I haven't seen you in weeks." A woman appeared suddenly. She was matronly, probably in her forties. She had a round, friendly face and the general demeanor of someone who was joyful about life.

"Hello, Martha." Wes took her hat off and held it in front of her chest.

"And who is this, pray tell?" Martha smiled broadly and looked Charlotte up and down.

"This is Charlotte. We…we met in St. Louis a while ago."

"You don't say." Martha's eyes sparkled with curiosity.

"It's very nice to meet you, Mrs. Miller." Charlotte extended her hand.

"You call me Martha, and that fellow over there is my other half, Wade." She held Charlotte's hand between both of hers and nodded with her head in Wade's direction, confirming Charlotte's initial thought about him. "I've been wanting those Holden boys to settle down. But this one would never let me fix him up. Now I see why." She winked at Charlotte.

Wes looked as if she'd seen a ghost, except that her cheeks were pink. It was clear that Martha was making Wes uncomfortable, and it was adorable.

"I got here as soon as I was able." Charlotte joined in Martha's fun.

"I'm so happy to meet you." Martha patted her hand. And then all of sudden Martha's expression changed. She grew serious. "Oh, my goodness, we had a coach get held up recently. You weren't a passenger on that stagecoach were you? The passengers didn't get off here. They only stopped for a minute at the livery, but the sheriff from Emporia said there was a woman on board and that she was missing."

"Oh, dear…I'm afraid that I should let someone know that I'm alright."

"It was you!" Martha fairly exclaimed.

All conversations stopped as the other patrons turned to look at them.

"Thank goodness you're not hurt. You poor sweet dear." Martha put her arm around Charlotte and ushered her to a nearby table.

Wes watched as Charlotte was swept away by Martha. She was left standing in the middle of the mercantile with her hat still in her hands as Martha served Charlotte some hot tea. Wade waved her over to where he stood behind the long counter. Shelves loaded with all manner of goods and supplies lined the wall behind him. Wade was talking to a man she didn't recognize. He was a stout fellow. He had a long beard and looked like a hunter or trapper, from the skins he'd made into boots and the long knife in the fringed sheath that hung from his wide belt.

"What was Martha hollering about?" asked Wade.

"My..." Wes wasn't sure how to describe their connection. "Charlotte was on that stagecoach that got robbed."

"The sheriff is looking for her then." Wade braced his hands on the counter. "She's lucky to be alive. They brought the bodies of the other two passengers through here in a wagon. They took them on to Emporia."

"We're headed to Emporia to visit the stage office." Wes set her hat on the counter. She didn't really want to get sucked into talking about the details of how Charlotte had come to be at her cabin. She tried to change the subject. "Is the circuit preacher around?"

"I heard the two fellows that got shot were part of the crew that robbed that train in Missouri." Wade ignored her question.

"How so?"

"They were taken out by some of their own gang." The fellow that Wes didn't know answered.

The world away from the territory was far and rarely heard from. In order to reach the frontier, news had to be of such widespread interest as to almost fall from heaven. Similarly, incidents of frontier life only leaked out if it was of a sensational nature such as an Indian attack or a stagecoach robbery. In those cases, news traveled fast. It made Wes feel uneasy that Charlotte had any part in this particular tragedy.

"Wes, this is Frank Stauven." Wade introduced them.

Wes tipped her head in greeting.

"Did they catch the men who did the shooting?"

"Far as I've heard, no," said Frank. There was a small stack of supplies in front of him on the counter. He began to gather them up in his arms. "I'd be on the lookout if I was you."

Wes nodded. A fist of nerves clenched in her stomach at the thought that Charlotte might still be in some sort of danger. Maybe it was better that everyone thought she was still missing. Wes wasn't sure.

"Do you know if the circuit preacher is around?" Wes asked again. The door banged behind her as Frank exited, causing her to jump. She glanced over at Charlotte, who was still chatting with Martha. Their eyes locked for a moment and the tightness in her stomach eased. Charlotte was okay, she was safe, and Wes was going to see that she stayed that way.

"Looking to tie the knot are ya?" Wade grinned at her.

"Yeah."

❖

Charlotte was grateful for the tea Martha had shared, but she was happy to be back on the wagon seat next to Wes. Martha was a chatterbox and had pelted her with questions. Charlotte had done her best to answer without revealing too much, but the woman was relentless in a good-natured, maternal sort of way.

Wes had learned from Wade that the circuit preacher was in Emporia, which they'd half expected. So, they would continue their journey and arrive at some point the next day. Luckily, she'd packed enough food and they'd brought blankets in case they needed to camp. Charlotte was a little nervous about sleeping in the open. But everything about this new adventure was less scary as long as Wes was by her side.

"I found out something about the ambush from Wade." Wes stared straight ahead as she spoke.

"You did?"

"It seems the men who were shot were actually wanted for a train robbery in Missouri. The fellows that held up the stage were part of their gang." Wes glanced at her. "They knew each other."

Thinking back, Charlotte did notice a sense of familiarity among the men who'd stopped the stage and the two who'd been seated across from her. It was curious that she hadn't thought of it since the attack. If the robbers knew the men, why did they cover their faces? Possibly because the men weren't the only passengers, and there was also the driver to consider.

The two men who'd been shot had joined the stage at a halfway point between Kansas City and Emporia and they'd had an aggressive energy about them that had made Charlotte uncomfortable the minute they boarded. But she'd chalked it up to her own nervousness about traveling alone. She should have listened to her intuition and gotten off the stage in Hollister that day. But then she'd never have met Wes. A wave of gratitude and relief surged through her system. She looped her arm through Wes's feeling suddenly affectionate. Wes looked down at her arm and then back at her. Their eyes met and Wes smiled.

"You're very lucky…" Wes didn't say more, but Charlotte could see there was more behind her concerned expression.

Charlotte shivered, despite the sun's warmth. She was very lucky indeed.

They continued heading east until the sun began to sink behind them. Wes pulled off the trail a ways and cleared a space for a cook fire. They'd brought a little kindling with them, but Wes ended up scouring the surrounding prairie for buffalo chips to keep the fire going. Charlotte was initially repulsed by the notion, but decided this was just one more aspect of the unknowable adventure she'd begun when she left the settled comforts of St. Louis.

Wes cut strips of venison and warmed them in a pan with some leftovers from Charlotte's potato stew. They rounded out the meal with a cup of coffee and a large slice of Maddie's sweet potato pie. It was strange to eat food from a woman she had yet to meet. Charlotte would remedy that when she returned to the farm.

Charlotte sat on a wooden box from the wagon so that she could keep her dress mostly off the ground. She sensed the horses nearby, hobbled and eating grass. She pulled the shawl around her shoulders and watched sparks from the fire rise and disappear in the darkness. There were so many stars. The sky was cloudless and it was as if she could sense the heavens in a way she'd never been able to understand before. The immensity of the firmament made her feel very small and frail. She hugged herself.

"Are you cold?" Wes was seated across from her on the ground. "No. I'm fine, thank you." She smiled at Wes. "I was just feeling momentarily overwhelmed by the night sky."

"It is a beautiful night." Wes's features were warmly lit by the firelight.

Wes had said that the night was beautiful, but she was looking at Charlotte when she said it. Charlotte felt her cheeks warm from Wes's intense gaze. What was happening to her? Was it simply friendly affection, or did she feel something more for Wes? Her emotions seemed to have large swings lately, and from time to time she felt she didn't even know herself.

"We should probably turn in." Wes stood and dusted debris and grass from her trousers. "I can put a tarp over the bed of the wagon, but since it's so clear maybe we should just leave it open."

"I'm fine with that." Charlotte set the coffee pot aside as Wes kicked dirt over the coals to smother them.

Wes set the box Charlotte had been seated on at the back of the wagon bed like a step to assist her in climbing up. Charlotte continually noticed how thoughtful Wes was. Charlotte wondered if she'd been treated badly her entire life to be so surprised by even the smallest kindness. That thought made her a little sad.

They pushed Charlotte's bag and the other items aside and spread blankets on the wooden wagon bed. They covered themselves with another blanket.

"You know, I've never camped before." Charlotte adjusted her folded shawl under her head as a pillow and settled back to look at the stars again.

"Really?"

"I never really knew my father and my mother moved to the city to find work when I was really young. I don't even remember the place we lived before that."

"Is your mother still in St. Louis?"

"No, she passed away when I was sixteen." Charlotte took a deep breath. She rarely thought of her mother, who'd suffered a long slow decline from a lung disorder. "I've been on my own since then."

Charlotte rotated to look at Wes, who was staring up at the night sky. Moonlight on her face was as faint as a waning candle.

"What about your parents? Are they in Tennessee?" They'd talked briefly about the journey Wes and Clyde had made from Tennessee, but never about Wes's family.

"No, they died when I was a kid. Clyde and I were taken in by my aunt and uncle."

"Did you have a happy childhood?"

"I think so, mostly. I know my kinfolks tried to make us feel welcome, but only your parents feel like home when you're a kid." Wes turned to face her. "It's hard to explain, but I never felt like I fit in…and I sure wasn't going to get married off and get stuck there."

"So, you left?"

Wes nodded.

"Was it hard to leave?" Charlotte remembered the nights of worry and doubt before she'd actually taken the stage west.

"It wasn't hard to leave, but the trip out was difficult." Wes paused. "We didn't really have any money or supplies to speak of and only one horse between the two of us. We picked up work along the way where we could find it."

"And one of those places was St. Louis."

"Yeah. We stayed there for a few months."

"Imagine if we'd met each other there."

"That would have been something." Wes smiled.

Yes, that would have been something.

They were quiet for a long time and Charlotte wondered if Wes was asleep. She wasn't sure.

"Good night, Wes," she whispered.

"Good night." Wes spoke without opening her eyes.

Wes thought about her time in St. Louis. So different from anything she'd known in Tennessee. A mere six miles from the ferry building where she worked unloading supplies and merchandise, the two great rivers joined into one. The wild waters of the frontier pouring into the bustling current of the everyday. It was the confluence of old and new, known and unknown, civilization and wilderness.

The Mississippi teemed with traffic. From the south, manufactured supplies moved upriver to the boom town of St. Louis, while downstream flowed the raw resources of the frontier. She'd heard stories of New Orleans and thought of traveling there, but the frontier's call felt more insistent. Even still, that didn't stop her from listening to the stories.

Wes was fascinated by the fur traders and voyagers. They'd tie their laden wooden boats at the ferry landing and sometimes even camp for the night. She marveled at their tales of savage native encounters, teeming game, the forever plains and the mountains beyond.

The frontier became an aching presence that she could feel but couldn't define. A magnetic force pulling her toward something that seemed bright and inevitable. She was certain that the frontier would offer her freedom from convention, a chance for new beginnings. Even if she had no sure sense of what either of those things looked like.

CHAPTER TWENTY-ONE

Wes stood several yards away from the wagon and sipped her coffee. The horizon was shifting from purple to pink, and the sun was about to show itself. There was nothing to block her view of the sunrise except miles of tall golden grass. She'd slept well. Ever since she'd shared her secret with Charlotte a peace had settled in her chest that she hardly recognized and didn't fully understand. Was it because of Charlotte or simply the relief of no longer hiding?

"There's a little coffee left. Would you like more?" Charlotte had carried the pot out to where she was standing.

"Sure. No need to waste coffee." Wes held out her cup for Charlotte.

"I was thinking…"

Wes sipped as she studied Charlotte's face.

"I was thinking that I'm probably due some sort of refund from the stage company. Since I never reached my destination." Charlotte held the pot in front of her using a cloth so as not to burn herself. "It wouldn't hurt to ask."

"You're probably right."

"Maybe we'd get enough to stay in a hotel and have something left over to pick up supplies." Charlotte seemed pleased with her plan. "I want to contribute in any way I can. And besides…tonight will be our wedding night." Her words carried playfulness as if she'd just shown the best foresight and they were the only two people in the world who knew it.

Wes smiled. If this was all just for show, why did she feel so nervous at the mention of sharing a hotel room?

"I think camping agrees with you." Wes turned to walk back to the wagon with Charlotte.

"I think all of this agrees with me." She had a serious expression when she looked at Wes.

She wasn't sure what to make of that comment from Charlotte, and instead of responding Wes busied herself with hitching the horses and packing up the wagon. In short order they were on their way again. It would only take a few more hours to reach Emporia. Wes hoped if they made good time they could take care of things and then be on the way back home by the following day. Wes was nervous to leave the claim unattended for too long. Too much could happen in a place that was so far from anywhere that no one would witness it.

❖

They passed more frame houses as they neared the growing settlement. Emporia was located in the Flint Hills region at the junction of the Cottonwood and Neosho Rivers. The entire area had originally been the home of the Kansa and Osage Indians. At least that was so until the 1840s, which was long before Wes arrived. By the time she and her brother staked a claim in Kansas, Emporia had already been declared an official town populated with white settlers.

Wes liked to know the history of a place. Every place had stories, and things usually went along more easily if you understood those stories. Not that the land itself could carry a grudge, but it did give off a feeling sometimes.

Her kinfolk back in Tennessee carried lots of stories, and many of them were anchored to a particular wooded gap between the hills or near an old grove of hardwoods or a granite outcropping. Any time Wes had visited those spots she could feel the story almost as if she'd witnessed it herself.

The oldest building in Emporia was a wood-framed structure on the northwest corner of 6th and Commercial streets. It was now a boarding house and occasionally served as the town's religious and governmental headquarters. There were other buildings that had sprung up over the years—the Hornsby and Fick store and the Emporia House Hotel. The stage ran regularly from Lawrence to Emporia, and it was there that Wes made the first stop.

She helped Charlotte down from the wagon and followed her up the steps of the stage office. Placards posted along the wall caught her attention. There was land for sale, wanted posters, pro-slavery posters, and warnings about Emporia's strict prohibition of alcohol. Wes had no desire to live in a community that could simultaneously be pro-slavery and against liquor.

A man and woman walked past Wes and stared. She stared back, wondering what they found so interesting. Emporia was a travel hub for all trails west, so it wasn't as if folks who lived here didn't see a lot of strangers. Perhaps she looked rougher than she realized. It wasn't as if she ever worried about what she looked like or what condition her clothes were in.

"Are you coming?" Charlotte had been standing in the open door waiting for her.

"Yeah, sorry."

The stage office was a busy place. There were several people in line so Charlotte and Wes had to wait to see a ticket agent. Wes removed her hat and ran her fingers through her hair, suddenly feeling self-conscious around so many strangers.

"You look fine." Charlotte touched her arm.

"I'm not so sure," Wes said in a hushed tone.

That made Charlotte smile. She smothered her laugh with her hand.

"Next!" the agent behind the counter called out, probably louder than necessary. But there was a fairly loud clatter of voices all around echoing off the wooden interior. He was a slender man, partially bald, probably in his thirties.

Wes stood behind Charlotte while she explained her situation. It was obvious from the agent's expression that he was shocked by her story and possibly more than a little relieved when Charlotte got to the ending.

"We had alerted the sheriff about you, miss. You don't know how happy I am to see you." He motioned for her to follow him. He walked from behind the counter and ushered them to an office.

A half hour later, after meeting with the station manager, Charlotte and Wes were finally on their way again. The stage company refunded the entire price of the ticket, which was a handsome sum. More money than Wes had ever seen in one place. Basically, more money than she'd made in a month working the docks in St. Louis.

"I think we should definitely treat ourselves to a bath and a hotel room tonight." Charlotte held up the hem of her skirt as they descended the stairs of the stage office. It seemed as if a weight had been lifted off her shoulders and her bright mood was contagious.

"Maybe we should take care of this wedding thing first." Wes replaced her hat when they reached the dirt road in front of the stage office. "I bet we'll find the preacher or a justice of the peace back at the old boarding house."

Charlotte nodded.

"We could walk from here and let the horses rest." The horses were tied at the front of the building near a water trough. "But I should probably take the rifle rather than leave it here."

That was the only item of real value Wes had brought and she couldn't afford to lose it.

CHAPTER TWENTY-TWO

Charlotte walked beside Wes along the dusty street toward the boarding house. She had butterflies in her stomach but was unsure of the cause exactly. Weddings were thresholds of change in a woman's life. She greeted this crossroad with a mixture of anticipation, excitement, and trepidation. She kept glancing over at Wes, but it was impossible to know what she was feeling. Was Charlotte the only one feeling nervous?

This whole thing had initially been her idea. Whether the nuptials were of a traditional nature or not, she and Wes were still binding themselves together for better or worse. That was not a thing to be taken lightly.

Emporia was a busy place and as it turned out, Wes and Charlotte weren't the only couple hoping to marry. Emporia was the last real town before traveling through the territory. Another couple had decided to seek the services of the justice of the peace before setting out on the Santa Fe Trail.

Wes and Charlotte stood quietly near the back of the room and listened to the murmured vows of the bride and groom.

"I just realized we don't have a ring." Wes whispered so that only Charlotte could hear.

"Yes, we do." Charlotte opened her small cloth bag and removed a change purse. In it she had carried her mother's ring all the way from St. Louis. "It was my mother's." Charlotte held the ring out to Wes in the palm of her hand.

"That's a nice ring."

Wes took it from Charlotte and held it between her fingers. The ring wasn't anything extravagant. A simple gold band with the delicate carving of leaves all around. It was the only real thing of value that Charlotte owned. And shortly after embarking on her trip West, she had thought she might have to barter or sell it if she got into trouble.

Wes tucked the ring into her shirt pocket just as the justice of the peace called to them from the front of the room. Wes set the rifle against the wall in the corner of the room for the ceremony.

There were two witnesses present for the ceremony, a young man who was the secretary to the justice of the peace and the wife of the owner of the boarding house. They stood stoically behind Wes and Charlotte as they faced each other. The officiant, Mr. Tanner, was cordial, but got right to the affair. He probably had a lot of other business besides weddings to attend to.

"Do you have a ring?" Mr. Tanner's question was directed at Wes.

"Yes, sir." Wes handed him the ring and Mr. Tanner laid it on the crease of the book he held in front of him.

"You may hold hands if you wish while you repeat the vows."

He was probably used to dealing with couples who were shy in public about their affections. Which was exactly how Charlotte suddenly felt. She'd expected Wes to be the shy one, but instead Wes seemed calm, at least outwardly. It was impossible to know what was really churning behind that intense gaze of hers.

Charlotte took a moment to commit the scene to memory. She noticed details about the room, a rustic space that someone had tried to elevate and soften with lamps and upholstered chairs and even a generously large sectional rug. She took notice of Wes as they held hands and faced each other. Wes was several inches taller than she was. With her broad shoulders and slim build Wes easily fit the image in her mind of the sort of fellow she'd pictured marrying. Wes had buttoned her collared shirt all the way to the top and she'd smoothed her hair back as best she could. Her forehead wasn't as tan as the rest of her face, probably having been shaded by the brim of her hat. Wes smiled at her and the nerves fluttered away.

"Place the ring on the finger of her left hand and repeat after me." He gave the ring back to Wes.

Wes slid the ring partway onto Charlotte's finger and held it there.

"Wesley Holden, do you take Charlotte Rose to be your wife?" Mr. Tanner's question was calm and fatherly in tone, as if he were trying to put them at ease.

"I do." Wes squeezed Charlotte's hands ever so lightly.

"Do you promise to love, honor, cherish and protect her, forsaking all others and holding only unto her?"

"I do." Wes took a deep breath.

Mr. Tanner nodded, indicating that Wes should set the ring in place. After sliding the small gold band the rest of the way, Wes returned to loosely holding her hands.

"Charlotte Rose, do you take Wesley Holden to be your husband?"

"I do." She wasn't sure she'd actually answered out loud, so she said it again a little louder. "I do."

"Do you promise to love, honor, cherish him, forsaking all others and holding only unto him?"

"I do."

"By the power invested in me by the territory of Kansas, I now pronounce you husband and wife." He closed the book and smiled at Wes. "You may kiss the bride."

The kiss! She hadn't thought of it until now.

Wes hesitated for a moment but then closed the space between them and kissed her tenderly on the lips. The kiss was but a fleeting touch, but somehow, she felt it all the way to her toes. A tingling tendril of electricity ran the length of her body and back in the blink of an eye. Heat rose to her cheeks instantly.

Wes paid Mr. Tanner for the service out of the cash they'd gotten for the ticket and they turned to leave. When they left the dim interior of the building Charlotte was sure that the sun was brighter and the air cleaner than she'd ever noticed before.

"Why don't we get a room at the hotel?" Wes's hand was lightly at her elbow as they walked toward the wagon. "You could get settled in while I take the horses to the livery for the night."

"That sounds good to me." The excitement of the day was catching up with her. Some time to rest and recharge sounded like a luxury.

The long hem of her skirt stirred dust as they walked toward the hotel. It was obvious that it hadn't rained in days, and a powdery brown film covered almost everything along the road from all the hoof traffic and handcarts. The porch railing along the front of the building, normally whitewashed, looked tan. If you touched any surface near an open window you'd leave a clean spot where your hand had been.

❖

At some point during the check-in process at the hotel, Wes realized that she should stop worrying about standing out or looking out of place. The truth was, hardly anyone gave her a second glance. Everywhere they went, all eyes were on Charlotte. She was like a colorful flower in a field of dry grass. Wes had certainly noticed how pretty Charlotte was, even the first time she laid eyes on her, with streaks of dirt down the side of her face. But today Charlotte practically glowed. She smiled at Wes as they climbed the stairs to their room. Wes was one step behind carrying Charlotte's bag and the rifle. Wes couldn't help smiling back.

"I'll order a bath for us if you like." Charlotte opened the door to the rented room on the second floor.

"That sounds nice."

"I packed a fresh shirt for you." Charlotte stepped into the room.

"You did?" Wes was touched that Charlotte had thought ahead about this.

The room was narrow and high ceilinged with a single window looking down on Commercial Street. An iron bed was placed long ways against the wall. And along the opposite wall was a dresser with a washbasin and a pitcher next to a wardrobe. An unpainted table and two straight chairs took up most of the remaining space. The water closet was two doors down the hall.

Wes was reluctant to leave Charlotte's side, but she knew she needed to tend to the horses, and the sooner she did that the sooner she could get back.

It took a half hour to walk Ned and Dusty to the livery and get them settled for the night. She returned to the hotel and took the steps two at a time until she reached the landing. Charlotte was just coming out of the water closet when Wes reached the door to their room.

"That was quick." Charlotte had changed out of her dress into a long robe from the closet in their room. "The bath is just now ready. Would you like to go first?"

"No, you should enjoy it, then I'll take a turn." Wes figured she was covered in a lot more dust than Charlotte. She didn't mind resting in the room for a little while. A lot had happened today, and she had a lot to get her mind around.

In the recesses of her mind, somewhere she hardly allowed thoughts to form, Wes had considered she might marry someday. But she also knew her situation was complicated. Even if she couldn't put her finger on exactly why. In any event, this wasn't exactly how she'd have pictured it even if she'd allowed herself to do so.

Maybe this was even better than she could have imagined. Charlotte could be a real friend, the partner she needed most. Without her brother, Wes might have existed in an isolated condition on the farm. It was true that it would have been nearly impossible to keep everything going all on her own. Meeting Charlotte had been a gift.

She sat in the chair by the window and slipped out of her dusty boots in anticipation of taking a bath. Her socks were almost as dusty as her boots. She beat them out against her leg. Little clouds of dirt puffed with every whack. Her jacket was next. The one that Charlotte had patched for her. She ran her fingertip over the tight, neat stitches. Wes hung it on a peg near the door then sat back down and waited. She slouched in the chair and closed her eyes, enjoying the moment of quiet.

CHAPTER TWENTY-THREE

The hot bath was a luxury. Especially since the tub was actually long enough and deep enough that Wes could sink until she was completely submerged. She'd lingered until the water was nearly room temperature. She figured she'd allowed Charlotte enough time to get ready alone in the room.

Wes had brought clothes in with her to change for dinner. She donned the clean shirt Charlotte had packed for her. Unfortunately, she had to wear the same trousers, but they didn't look too bad. Wes combed her damp hair to one side. She did her best to make a straight part with the comb, although she wasn't sure she succeeded. Then she slicked it back. She studied herself in the mirror as she buttoned the last button at her collar.

She felt like a different person somehow and she wasn't sure exactly why. She slipped her arms into her brother's navy wool vest and decided she looked quite dapper. This may have been the most dressed up she'd ever gotten.

Wes rolled her discarded shirt and undergarments together into a tight bundle and tucked it under her arm. She tapped lightly on the door to their room. She didn't want to surprise Charlotte if she was still getting ready.

Charlotte opened the door and smiled.

"Don't you look handsome."

"You look very nice too." That sounded like a weak compliment, despite her sincerity. Wes decided to step outside her comfort zone a bit more. "What I meant to say was, you look beautiful."

Charlotte seemed pleased with Wes's assessment. She looked away for an instant and color rose to her cheeks.

"Shall we go downstairs for dinner?" Charlotte relieved Wes of her bundle of clothing and then closed the door to their room. She joined Wes in the hallway. She slipped her arm through Wes's as they descended the stairs to the main level of the hotel.

As they reached the lobby, a man stood and approached them.

"I wondered if I might have a word with you." He held his hat in front of him. Wes noticed the badge on his coat lapel right away. "I'm Sheriff Billings and I was hoping to speak with Charlotte Rose."

"Charlotte Rose Holden." Charlotte politely corrected him.

"Yes, of course." He tipped his head. "My congratulations to the happy couple."

"What's this about?" Wes was feeling protective and as the husband in this scenario thought it best to act that way.

"The stage office notified me and relayed your story." He paused briefly. "I was hoping Miss Charlotte might be able to identify the men who robbed the stagecoach."

"I'm sorry, but I'm sure the station agent told you that the men had their faces covered. And it all happened so quickly."

"I understand." He seemed disappointed.

"I'm sorry I can't be more helpful."

"That's alright, ma'am." He held his hat in one hand and rested his other on the gun holstered on his belt. "The important thing is you're alright." He nodded and took a step back. "If you do happen to remember anything, my office is just down the street from the hotel. I'll let you get on with your evening."

With that, he turned and put his hat on as he exited the hotel.

Once again, Wes was reminded of how close Charlotte had come to disaster. She ushered Charlotte into the dining room. They stood for a moment until the hostess directed them to a table. The dining room wasn't huge, but it was the largest, nicest room Wes had ever dined in. Each table was draped with white table linen and the walls were covered with a printed wallpaper, or maybe it was a large drapery. In any event, it seemed like a nice place and Wes felt a bit out of her element. She'd never experienced finery. In fact, she'd never stayed in a hotel before. Maybe Charlotte hadn't either, but she'd worked in one. So, she definitely seemed more at ease in these surroundings.

"Is something wrong?" Charlotte must have sensed her internal doubts.

"No, I'm fine." Wes mimicked Charlotte by placing the napkin across her lap. "I've just never been in a place quite this fancy."

"Well, I think you fit in perfectly here." Charlotte sounded like she truly meant it.

They ordered food and the smell of something savory wafted from the kitchen. Wes realized she was famished.

"Here you go." The woman who'd taken their dinner order returned with two plates heaped with food, and one small bowl of what looked like buttery mashed potatoes. "Let me know if I can bring you anything else."

Charlotte watched Wes from across the table as the matronly woman set plates of food in front of them.

"Thank you." For some reason, Charlotte felt like a schoolgirl around this older woman, like a kid under the measuring eye of a stern schoolmarm. Probably because she felt as if this entire evening was one big adventure and that any moment they could be found out. But that didn't seem likely. She felt truly happy as she watched Wes dig into her meal.

The dinner consisted of a generous slice of salted pork, thick sliced bread, and beans. Charlotte slathered butter on a piece of the bread and paired that with the first taste of the pork. It was savory and quite good. As she chewed she surveyed the room. There were probably ten or twelve other people in the dining area, all at various stages of their meal. Some had obviously arrived earlier and now sat drinking coffee and chatting. The rough-hewn boards of the floor and the pine paneling on the ceiling made the space a little loud. There were no soft surfaces to absorb sound, except for the patrons themselves.

The warm meal and darkness outside the windows were making her tired. She covered a yawn with her napkin. Charlotte knew the minute they traveled to their quarters for the night, she'd probably collapse. She tried to rally. She didn't really want the day to be over.

After coffee and desert, which consisted of a delicious custard pie, Charlotte declared that she couldn't eat one more bite.

She and Wes climbed the stairs to their rented room for the night. Wes opened the door and let Charlotte step in first. After putting her shawl over the chair, Charlotte excused herself to the water closet. When she returned, Wes hadn't moved. She was standing in the center of the small room as if she were waiting for directions of what to do next.

Charlotte sat on the chair and unfastened her shoes while Wes took a turn in the washroom. Charlotte took notice of how small the bed was while she waited for Wes. She didn't want to change clothes until Wes was back and they were locked in for the night.

They turned away from each other to undress like bashful teenagers. Once Charlotte was in her nightgown she climbed on the bed, taking the position closest to the wall. Wes was wearing a long nightshirt that hung to her knees. Wes blew out the candle on the nightstand and then joined Charlotte under the covers.

They lay side by side in bed looking up at the ceiling, like two schoolgirls having a sleepover. Charlotte wondered what Wes was thinking. Was she thinking the same things that Charlotte was?

Charlotte was dreaming of the life they would create for themselves and the baby. She knew that what they'd done today was an act of hope and trust. Charlotte was trusting Wes with her fate and the fate of her baby. That was no small thing. And as she lay next to Wes she was acutely aware of the warmth of Wes's body. Their shoulders were pressed against each other on the narrow bed so that she could feel the lean muscles of Wes's upper arm.

Sounds drifted from the street through the partially open window. The creak of wagon wheels passing over the uneven dirt road. The sound of a horse neighing in the distance. And somewhere a dog barked.

"Are you sleepy?" Charlotte whispered in the dark.

"Not really."

"Me either." Charlotte rolled onto her side to face Wes. "I'm tired, but I think I'm too excited to sleep."

They were quiet for a minute or two.

"Tell me a story." Charlotte wanted to know everything there was to know about Wes and she felt she'd only just scratched the surface. "Tell me something about Tennessee. I've never been there."

"I don't really know what you'd like to hear."

"Anything, I'd just like to listen to you talk."

Wes was quiet for a moment, no doubt trying to figure out what to say.

"Tennessee is very green in the summer. Where we lived there were mountains and rolling hills. Lots of hardwoods that in the fall turn all sorts of gold and red and orange."

"It sounds nice."

"We had a wide creek near our family's place, and it had a nice swimming hole." Wes took a breath. "My brother taught me to swim one summer."

"Tell me more about your family."

Wes was quiet again as if she were trying to decide what to share.

"My grandfather was a preacher." Wes paused. "He'd farm small plots in the hollows of the hills, corn and potatoes mostly, and then he'd preach on Sundays. He was a big man. Folks gave him a nickname. They called him Bear Joe."

Charlotte waited for Wes to continue.

"He had a temper. I was always sort of afraid of him. I'm not sure which would be worse, the wrath of God or his wrath, but I tried to avoid both." Even in the moonlight, Charlotte could see that Wes was smiling. "He liked to pull a cork too. And on those occasions, he liked to play the fiddle and my grandmother would hold my hands and we'd dance."

The bed creaked as Wes shifted.

"My grandparents' place was in a gap, shaded on all sides by mountains. The place was so green in the summer. So many hardwoods and you could grow anything. There was always plenty of rain." Wes paused. "Thinking back, I didn't realize how easy life was. In some ways, but not in others."

"You mean because of losing your folks?"

"Yeah, and my grandparents passed that same year." She paused. "It was losing family and just realizing as I got older I couldn't quite find my place."

Wes was still lying on her back and Charlotte scooted closer, resting her head on Wes's shoulder. She laid her palm on Wes's forearm and brushed her fingertips lightly over Wes's warm skin.

"I think I know what you mean." Charlotte didn't completely understand. She'd never really felt out of place exactly, but she'd also never felt quite settled. She'd been searching for more but not exactly sure where to find it. Maybe she finally had. She squeezed Wes's arm and closed her eyes.

"Good night, Wes."

"Good night, Charlotte."

CHAPTER TWENTY-FOUR

W es woke at first light. They hadn't drawn the curtains and a soft pink hue warmed the room. They'd slept spooned against each other. Charlotte was snuggled against Wes's stomach and her hair lightly tickled Wes's face. Her arm was around Charlotte's waist and the palm of her hand rested on the low curve of Charlotte's stomach. The intimacy of their embrace surprised her, but even as the cobwebs of slumber lifted, she didn't pull away. Wes took a moment to savor the closeness. She took a deep breath and inhaled the scent of rose water and some other pleasing scent she couldn't put her finger on, possibly lavender.

She slid her hand slowly across Charlotte's stomach. The fabric of Charlotte's nightgown was thin, and as she moved her hand she brushed the underside of Charlotte's breasts. Wes would have immediately withdrawn her hand, except Charlotte covered it. And then she entwined her fingers with Wes's and snuggled closer.

Was Charlotte still asleep? Wes wasn't sure and she tried to relax, but some ache deep inside was throbbing in unison with her heartbeat. She couldn't quite settle no matter how hard she tried.

After a few moments, Charlotte stirred. She released Wes's hand and smothered a yawn. Wes took the opportunity to roll over onto her back. It wasn't that she wanted to bolt out of bed, but her insides were in a flurry and she wasn't exactly sure why. She kept her eyes closed and waited to see what might happen next.

"Wes, are you awake?" Charlotte whispered the question as she draped her arm over Wes's midsection.

"Sort of," she answered without opening her eyes.

"I'm sorry, I need to visit the water closet." There was a bit of urgency in Charlotte's statement.

Wes rolled out of bed so that Charlotte could make her escape. Charlotte pulled on a robe over her nightgown and checked the hallway, looking side to side, before she darted from the room. Wes relaxed back in bed and took a deep breath. After several minutes, Charlotte returned.

Before Wes could get out of bed, Charlotte was climbing across her.

"How did you sleep?" Charlotte was straddling her stomach with her arms braced on each side of Wes.

"Good." Wes swallowed. "How about you?"

"Very good." Charlotte continued her climb to the other side of the bed and flopped onto her back. "I can't tell you how wonderful it is to stay in a hotel instead of work in one. It's a luxury to use a chamber pot that I know I won't have to empty."

"I've never even been in a hotel before this one." Wes felt as if her life since meeting Charlotte had been one new discovery after another about the world and about herself. "Should we get some breakfast before we head back?"

"Yes." Charlotte sat up and swept her fingers through her hair. "I'm starving."

Wes got out of bed and slid her trousers on under her nightshirt. She was about to sweep the shirt off over her head but suddenly suffered a bout of bashfulness. She rotated away from Charlotte and reached for the wrap that she wore to cover her breasts. It wasn't that her breasts were very noticeable, but she felt safer with the extra layer of cloth beneath her undershirt. In her hurry to dress she was having trouble getting the cloth wrapping to lay flat.

"Can I help you with that?"

Charlotte's question carried nothing but kindness, yet Wes still felt more exposed than she liked. She'd never let anyone see something so private. And she couldn't even find her voice to answer, but she allowed Charlotte to take the thin cloth from her hand. Charlotte was respectful enough to stand behind her and only assisted with the part that covered her back, then passed the strand of loose cloth to Wes so that she could cover herself in the front. Once finished, Wes tugged on her undershirt. Only then did she turn to look at Charlotte.

Charlotte was looking up at her with the sweetest expression and Wes had the strongest urge to kiss her, or hold her, or both. But she hesitated and, in that moment, Charlotte reached for her dress on the chair.

"I'll go freshen up and leave you to get dressed." Wes looked away and hurried out the door to the washroom.

❖

Breakfast was a casual affair consisting of eggs, toast, and coffee. After eating, Charlotte packed their bag while Wes carried the rifle along as she retrieved the horses from the livery. As Wes led the team back down the street, she could see Charlotte standing on the steps waiting. Just the sight of Charlotte's smiling face made Wes's heart flutter.

She climbed down from the wagon and tied the horses to the post out front.

"I was thinking we should pick up a few supplies when we get to Hollister." Wes took the satchel from Charlotte and set it in the wagon next to the rifle.

"That sounds fine to me." Charlotte accepted Wes's hand as she stepped up to the high front seat.

"We might want to pick up a can of beans or some corn cakes for tonight since we'll need to camp again." Wes hoisted up to the seat beside Charlotte. She shook the reins as a signal to Ned and Dusty to walk forward. "I could get just enough for dinner down the street at the old market house and we can pick the rest up from the mercantile in Hollister."

"I like that plan." Charlotte smiled.

Was it just Wes's imagination, or did Charlotte look different somehow? She had a certain glow about her face. Wes couldn't help smiling back.

Wes pulled the horses to a stop in front of the market at the far end of town and handed the reins to Charlotte, and then set the brake against the wheel. Charlotte regarded her with wide eyes.

"I don't know anything about handling horses."

"Don't worry." Wes jumped down. "I'll be back before they notice I'm gone."

CHAPTER TWENTY-FIVE

It had been nearly a week since the trip to Emporia. Charlotte had been enjoying the rhythm of daily life with Wes. Each day began as soon as the sun was up and ended just after dark. She was tired at the end of each day, but it was a very different sort of exhaustion than what she'd felt in St. Louis. Working the farm meant that she immediately and personally benefited from all her labors. This was a very satisfying existence.

On this particular day Charlotte had decided it was time to meet her neighbors. She'd been curious about Ben's wife, Maddie, ever since he'd delivered the sweet potato pie. Charlotte had purchased two jars of berry preserves before leaving Emporia and she intended to give one of them to Maddie to break the ice. It seemed that Maddie was the only other woman close to her age anywhere nearby, so she hoped to strike up a friendship. Charlotte settled the jar into a basket and covered it with a cloth.

Wes was walking toward the cabin as she stepped outside.

"I can take a break and give you a ride over to the Caufield place." Wes removed her hat and wiped her forehead with her shirtsleeve. It was late morning and the sun was well up and warm.

"I'm happy to walk." She didn't want Wes to lose too much time away from work just because she wanted to make a social call.

"I'm just a little worried. It's easy to get turned around out here. The landscape all looks the same." Wes replaced her hat and braced her hands on her hips. She sounded more concerned than controlling, so Charlotte decided to relent.

"Maybe you're right."

"Once you get there and know where it is, you can always walk home if you feel up to it." Wes turned toward the barn. "It'll just take me a minute to hitch the team."

Charlotte stood in the shadow of the cabin and enjoyed the view of the field they'd just cleaned. They'd pruned and weeded and nursed the plants into a fine condition. She was proud of the work she'd done. She was learning a lot and Wes was a great teacher. Of course, they did have a division of labor that also suited her skills. Half the day she kept to the house to cook, do laundry, and sew. She'd been trying to make the cabin cozier, with a few more creature comforts. She'd picked up some cloth in Hollister for curtains and had even gotten material for a new dress. She would need something new to wear soon that could accommodate the baby growing inside her, but for now, the bump was barely showing. That would probably change soon.

Luckily, the morning sickness had passed.

Wes returned. She walked the team to the house and assisted Charlotte into the wagon.

"How far is it to their farm?"

"Hmm, probably four miles." Wes snapped the reins and the wagon lurched forward. "It's a nice walk, but if you're not home by dusk I'll ride over and get you okay?"

"Thank you." She had no idea what Maddie would be like or if she'd linger. "Have you met Maddie before?"

"Yeah."

"What's she like?"

"She's nice."

Charlotte laughed.

"What's so funny?"

"You." Charlotte looped her arm through Wes's. "Getting information out of you is like pulling teeth."

"Well, it's not like Maddie and I have ever sat around having *girl talk*." Wes smirked.

"No, I suppose not." Charlotte smiled.

❖

Charlotte wasn't sure how far four miles was, but it did seem that they'd been following the narrow trail south for quite a while. Finally, a wisp of smoke was visible on the horizon and then soon after, the dark shape of a house. Ben was out in the field with a small boy. He waved to them as they passed. He was too far away to hear them if they called out to him. The boy was dragging a rake of some kind.

As they drew closer to the cabin, a woman appeared in the doorway. She shielded her eyes from the sun. After a minute she must have recognized Wes because she waved and walked in their direction. A little girl hovered around her long skirt, mostly hiding but clearly curious.

"Hello, Maddie." Wes climbed down and then circled the wagon to assist Charlotte from the other side.

"Hi, Wes." Maddie wiped her hands on her apron and then smoothed it down. Her expression grew serious as she stepped closer. "I was very sorry to hear about your brother."

"Thank you." The sadness was evident in Wes every time Clyde was mentioned.

"Hello, I'm Maddie Caufield." She smiled. "You must be Charlotte."

"Yes, it's so nice to finally meet you."

Maddie was petite, like Charlotte, with wavy dark hair down to her shoulders. She tied it away from her face with a ribbon like a schoolgirl. Her skin was fair, and she had dark brown eyes. There was a girlish innocence about Maddie that might have inspired feelings of protectiveness in Charlotte, almost like an older sister would want to look after a younger sister even though she suspected they were close to the same age. Her daughter's hair was a lighter brown. She took after her father. Maddie had a very pleasing calmness about her.

"This is my daughter, Rachel."

"It's nice to meet you, Rachel."

Rachel shyly ducked behind her mother's long skirt again, Maddie touched Rachel's hair and soothed her with whispered words that Charlotte couldn't quite make out.

"I hope you'll both stay for a visit." Maddie looked past them in search of Ben. "Ben is out there working somewhere, but I'm sure he'd take a break."

"Nah, don't bother him." Wes shook her head. "I have to get back anyway."

"Well, I hope at least you might stay for a little while?" Maddie looked at Charlotte.

"I would love to if it's not an imposition."

"Please, I never…and I do mean *never* have company." Maddie smiled. "You are a rare treat in a land full of men." She turned to Wes. "No offense meant."

"None taken." Wes grinned and touched her hat. "I'll leave you two to get acquainted."

Maddie and Charlotte turned toward the house as Wes pointed the wagon toward home. Charlotte looked back to wave good-bye, but Wes seemed distracted with the horses.

"I'm so pleased that you came for a visit." Maddie looped her arm through Charlotte's. "I've been hoping you would ever since Ben mentioned that he met you."

Charlotte followed Maddie into the cabin. It was similar in some ways to Wes's place. One larger room that served as kitchen and living space with a stone fireplace at one end. Then two smaller bedrooms set off from the main room. It was clear that Maddie had had more time to improve the homeyness of the place. There was a rug on the wood floor and colorful napkins and towels on the kitchen table.

"Come, sit down and I'll make us some tea." Maddie opened a small wooden box near the wash basin. "I have some nice herbs for tea."

"That would be lovely." Charlotte set her basket on the table and then remembered why she'd brought it. "I have a small gift for you."

"Oh, that wasn't necessary."

"It's a little thing, really." Charlotte held the jar of jam out to Maddie. "Just something to thank you for the pie. Which was delicious."

"I'm so happy you enjoyed it." Maddie admired the jam. "We should taste this."

Rachel seemed very excited by that suggestion. She stood at the end of the table and rested her chin at the edge between her tiny hands. Maddie set a pot to boil over the fire for hot water and then motioned for Charlotte to sit. In no time, cups of steaming tea sat in front of them, and Maddie had warmed a few biscuits from their morning meal so that they could each sample the jam.

Charlotte was pleased to discover that the jam tasted as good as it looked. The blackberry preserves were perfectly sweet.

"Can I have more?" Rachel had eaten the first half of her biscuit with gusto.

"Please?" Maddie looked at Rachel.

"May I please have more?"

"That's better." Maddie served a bit more jam onto the second half of Rachel's biscuit. "Now, why don't you go outside and play while the grownups talk?"

Rachel nodded as she took a huge bite. She skipped out the open door into the sunlight and was gone.

"If I had only half her energy..." Maddie let the statement trail off as she sipped her tea.

Charlotte considered telling Maddie that she was pregnant. She wanted to ask Maddie a lot of questions about kids and motherhood and what it was like to have a baby way out on the edge of nowhere. But she tamped down the queue of questions. They'd only just met and she thought perhaps that would be way too much personal information to share during a first meeting.

"How is Wes doing?" Maddie held her cup with both hands and looked at Charlotte over the rim. "I know he and his brother were very close. In fact, I've rarely seen Wes without Clyde."

"I think it's been hard for...him." Charlotte had to remind herself to use the right pronoun. "Unfortunately, I arrived after... the accident."

"So sad." Maddie shook her head. "He was a good man." She paused. "I didn't talk to either of them as much as Ben, but seeing as how they were our closest neighbors, well, we've helped each other out."

"I'm very happy that you are nearby. Having another woman so close makes me feel a little less lonely, even though we only just met." Charlotte wanted to change the subject away from Clyde. If Maddie asked too many questions it would be obvious that she didn't really know Clyde. Their cover story was that Charlotte and Wes met in St. Louis so it would also follow that Charlotte met Clyde there too. Better to redirect the conversation to the here and now. Once she knew Maddie better maybe she'd tell her the real story about how she'd nearly been shot, showed up at Wes's cabin and threatened her with a frying pan.

It was a miracle that everything had worked out the way it had. And sometimes she had to pinch herself just to be sure it was real.

"I feel the same way." Maddie reached across the table and patted her hand. "When Ben came home and told me a woman was on the place with Wes I almost danced a jig."

Charlotte laughed.

"I have to be honest, I feel a little out of my element," Charlotte said.

"You'll be fine." Maddie sounded so sure. "It does take some getting used to, the solitude…and Lord knows Ben is not the best conversationalist, but now that you're here we can visit from time to time."

"I'd really like that."

Charlotte took another bite of the jam covered biscuit and then studied it seriously.

"Now, please tell me how do you get these biscuits to brown so nicely."

Maddie smiled at the compliment.

"Butter is the key. I'll send some home with you."

CHAPTER TWENTY-SIX

W es decided after returning to the cabin to go hunting. This time for real. Their meat supply was getting lower than she liked. She unhitched the team, shouldered the rifle, and followed the creek north on foot until she saw some deer sign. Fresh tracks along the creek bank told her she'd probably just missed them.

She knelt for a minute and took several sips of water from the creek in her cupped hand. She waited for a spell, closed her eyes, and listened to the pleasing sound of the water babbling before she started walking again. As she walked and studied the ground for more tracks, Wes took note of the fact that she felt at peace.

The feeling had sort of gradually come over her at some point in the last several days. Yes, she'd worried about Charlotte a little ever since talking to the sheriff in Emporia, but she didn't mind leaving the cabin unattended now because she knew Charlotte was safe with Ben and Maddie. But aside from that small bit of worry, Wes felt happy. Her brother's absence still took up space in her heart, but other feelings were taking up residence too. Having Charlotte around had brightened her day-to-day existence in so many ways. In ways she didn't know were lacking until Charlotte filled them.

Maybe Ben and Maddie would become closer as neighbors now that Charlotte was here too. Wes knew she had a tendency to be standoffish with folks who weren't her kin. A holdover from her upbringing in the Appalachian hill country of Tennessee. And the need to keep her distance for fear of revealing her true self.

A solitary doe's ears popped up above the tall grass just ahead and Wes quickly sank to her knee. She'd been so lost in thought that she'd almost walked right up on the deer. Another few yards and she'd have spooked it into a run.

She held the heavy, long rifle aloft, sighted the doe, exhaled to steady herself, and then pulled the trigger.

❖

Wes carried the small doe across her shoulders all the way back to the cabin, with the rifle strap slung across her chest. She was winded from the effort of it all. She'd field-dressed the animal, slitting her neck and removing the entrails before returning to the house. She let the deer fall next to the fire pit. The animal landed in an unnatural pose, different from her grace in life.

She set the rifle aside and got to work building a fire to smoke the meat.

Wes set four stakes in the ground so as to form a square about four feet from the ground. She split forks in the tops and laid poles longways. She cut the raw meat into thin strips, salted them, and then hung each strip across the poles to smoke. Under the framework, she worked to keep the fire small to dry and smoke the meat, careful not to let it get hot enough to actually cook.

The goal was to dehydrate the strips of venison to cure them for longevity. Her brother had always told her that the best fuel for this purpose was birch. Especially black birch because it infused the dried meat with a pleasant flavor.

She stepped back to admire her afternoon of work.

A light breeze had arrived so she decided to set a windbreak using two long sticks and the canvas tarp from the wagon. She'd have to keep the fire going for another two to four hours to completely cure the meat. By then, Charlotte would be back, or she'd head over to the Caufield place with the wagon to fetch her.

Wes drew a bucket of water from the well. She sloshed water onto her hands and rubbed them together to remove the blood. Then she tipped the bucket to her mouth and took a long drink, allowing water to slosh out on either side soaking the front of her shirt.

❖

It was late afternoon when Charlotte started walking back home. Maddie and Rachel had escorted her until they could see the smoke from the cabin on the horizon. Charlotte said good-bye with a promise to visit again soon. True to her word, Maddie had sent Charlotte home with a little tub of fresh churned butter in her basket. She couldn't wait to share the special treat with Wes at dinnertime.

The late afternoon sky was beautiful. White, fluffy clouds sat on the horizon to the east. The rounded edges had the slightest hint of pink from the sinking sun to the west. Charlotte took a moment to savor the enormity of the landscape.

The grassland between where she stood and the small shape of the cabin swayed in undulating waves like the sea. Charlotte had never seen the ocean, but sometimes she wondered if the never-ending prairie felt similar. There was nothing but grass all around. Wind rippled across it and every gust changed the angle of the tall grass to the sun. Golden yellow turned to brown and then back again. The brightest yellow of the alternating colors seemed to reflect the light back at her like ripples of sunlight on water. Flecks of tiny plant debris set free by the breeze drifted and hovered in shafts of afternoon sunlight.

Charlotte started walking again. Her skirt rustled in the tall grass at each edge of the trail.

As she drew closer she could see that the tendril of whitish smoke they'd seen from a distance was actually near the barn where Wes was at work. Wes looked up and waved to her as she approached. But what was that all over Wes's clothing? It looked like blood!

She broke into a run until she was close enough to see Wes's face. She came to an abrupt stop with a hand on each of Wes's arms.

"Are you hurt?" Her heart pounded in her chest as she searched for any site of injury. Wes's shirt and trousers were a mess, covered in swaths of red-brown stains.

"No, no…I'm fine." Wes tried to sooth her. "I was curing meat. I went hunting while you were away."

"Oh, thank goodness." Relief flooded Charlotte's system. Her emotions were so easily tipped to the extreme these days.

"I'm sorry I scared you. I figured it was best to do all this while you weren't here since you couldn't even stomach the sight of a dead snake." Wes teased her.

Charlotte playfully swatted Wes's arm.

"I'll fill the bath for you if you're finished."

"Yeah, the messy part is over. I just need to allow it to smoke for another couple of hours."

It was a warm night so they left the tub near the well for ease. Charlotte set the wash pot over a fire near the tub to heat water for both bathing and laundry. Wes's clothing was so disgusting that she didn't even want Wes to step into the cabin wearing any of it.

"Give me those clothes and I'll wash them now."

The sun was low. As it fell behind the tree line along the creek it cast long shadows.

"You're getting so bossy." Wes smiled as she began to unbutton her shirt. She turned away as she slipped out of her clothing and into the tub. Wes was still a little bashful around Charlotte, but the simple fact that she would soak in a tub with Charlotte so near was a huge step.

Charlotte looked away until she heard the slosh of Wes sinking into the tub. When she turned around only Wes's broad shoulders were visible as she rested her arms along the edge of the tub. Charlotte used a stick to transfer Wes's discarded clothing into the wash pot over the fire. Then she used the wooden paddle to submerge the soiled clothing into the steaming water. She stirred it around a bit and then left it to soak.

"I could wash your hair if you like," Charlotte said.

In the waning evening light, the firelight painted Wes's shoulders with a warm glow. It took a minute for Wes to answer, and Charlotte worried she'd overstepped.

"Okay, that'd be nice." Wes half turned, but didn't look at Charlotte.

Charlotte took the pitcher she'd used to transfer the hot water to the bath. She handed it to Wes so that she could fill it from the tub while she remained behind her, to offer as much privacy as possible. Charlotte slowly poured the warm water over Wes's head. Then she lathered soap between her hands and gently worked her fingers through Wes's hair. At one point, Wes let the weight of her head fall into Charlotte's hands. Wes's eyes were closed, and in the near darkness the firelight created quite an intimately romantic scene.

Charlotte took a deep breath and continued to caress Wes's hair. She wanted this to last as long as possible. She'd longed for this sort of closeness ever since they'd shared the bed in the hotel. She wasn't sure if Wes had intentionally held her during the night, or if it had been an innocent accident, but Charlotte had discovered that she enjoyed it. And she wanted to feel the warmth of Wes's embrace again, she just wasn't sure how to communicate that to Wes.

Was Wes feeling the same twinges of affection that she was feeling? It was very hard to tell what Wes was thinking or feeling.

CHAPTER TWENTY-SEVEN

Wes would have allowed Charlotte to run her fingers through her hair all night. The sensation of Charlotte's caress was so unexpected. Emotion rose to her throat and lodged itself there so that when Charlotte spoke to her, Wes's response came out all raspy.

"Thank you." Wes sank as far as possible into the water.

"I could give you a haircut tomorrow if you like."

Wes nodded, unable to find her voice.

"Maybe I'll start dinner while you finish up." She heard Charlotte stir the laundry behind her. "I have a surprise for you, from Maddie."

"I'll be out in a minute." Wes sloshed warm water onto her shoulders.

"Take your time. The biscuits will take a little while."

Wes sat in the tub until the tips of her fingers were soft. Candlelight from the interior of the cabin spilled outside but didn't cover the spot where she soaked. She stepped out onto the grass and wrapped a blanket around her shoulders, then went inside to dress.

She slid the quilt across her sleeping area and searched for a clean shirt and trousers. It was warm so she decided to only wear a shirt without the wrapping or undergarment underneath. She felt a little exposed, but safe with Charlotte at the same time. When she slid the quilt back Charlotte was just setting plates of food on the table. The smell of warm biscuits filled the air reminding her of how hungry she was.

Wes finger combed her hair as she stood a few feet away from the table.

"You look great." Charlotte smiled. "I hope you're hungry."

"Starved." Wes took a seat. "Is that what I think it is?"

"Yes. Fresh butter." Charlotte sat down across from her. "Maddie and Ben have a cow. Could we have a cow some day?"

"I think that's a fine idea." Wes took a bite out of one of the biscuits. "Mmm, this is so much better than cornbread."

They both laughed.

It was a huge bonus that Charlotte was such a good cook. Wes had grown very tired of her own cooking and her brother Clyde's skills had been even worse.

After dinner, Charlotte cleaned up while Wes gathered the dried venison and doused the fire. Once she'd stored the meat, Wes settled on the stoop to smoke. She'd taken up smoking on the trek westward, although Wes hadn't taken out the pipe since her brother's passing. It seemed a strange and lonesome pastime without her brother.

She was lost in thought when Charlotte spoke from the doorway.

"Do you mind if I join you?"

"Please do." Wes slid over on the step to give Charlotte room to sit down.

"I didn't know you smoked."

"Ah, yeah, most men smoke…so, I thought it helped if I did too."

"I suppose you're right. I never really thought about it."

Wes puffed and blew circles into the darkness.

"Can I try?" Charlotte asked.

"Are you sure?"

Charlotte nodded, so Wes handed her the pipe. It had a rather long smooth stem in contrast to the hand-hewn bowl. Her brother had bartered for it on her behalf back in Missouri. She watched as Charlotte took tiny puffs, followed predictably by a fit of coughing.

Wes tried not to laugh. Charlotte waved smoke away from her face as she handed the pipe back to Wes.

"Not your cup of tea?"

Charlotte was still coughing so all she could do was shake her head.

After a little while, Charlotte's voice returned.

"Look. A shooting star." She pointed to the south.

"It's something isn't it?"

"What?"

"The night sky." Wes puffed thoughtfully. "Heaven."

"Do you think we can see heaven from here?"

Wes shrugged.

"I'd like to think we could." Charlotte kept staring up at the stars.

After a few minutes, Wes changed the subject. She wasn't really in the mood to think of those that had gone on. She was more interested in the present.

"How did you and Maddie get on?" She hadn't really had a chance to ask about the visit.

"Maddie is quite nice." Charlotte smiled. "I liked her a lot. I hope we can be friends."

"Who wouldn't want to be friends with you?" Wes found Charlotte fairly irresistible these days.

"You mean that?" Charlotte turned to her.

"Unless you're swinging a frying pan." Charlotte's expression had been so serious that Wes couldn't help teasing her.

"Oh, you!" Charlotte bumped Wes's shoulder with hers, almost knocking her off the narrow stoop. "I wasn't sure if you were dangerous or not."

"And now what do you think?" Wes arched her eyebrow.

"Oh, yes, you are definitely dangerous."

The low timbre of Charlotte's voice spoke volumes and warmed Wes's insides. Was she playing with fire here? Perhaps. Something was changing between them, and Wes had to admit that she liked it. Before Wes could say more, Charlotte closed the space between them and kissed her on the cheek.

"Good night, Wesley Holden." Charlotte stood and then disappeared inside the cabin, leaving Wes sitting alone on the steps.

Wes's heart felt all light and fluttery in her chest. She took a deep breath. She rotated to look inside the house, but Charlotte had already drawn the quilt across her bedroom for the night. Wes sat for a while longer. She closed her eyes and remembered the simultaneously soothing and unsettling sensation of Charlotte's fingers in her hair. She wasn't sure if she was nearly as dangerous as Charlotte.

Charlotte made her want things she'd never even considered before. Maybe that wasn't a bad thing. She just had to get used to the feelings and let her mind sit with them a while.

Wes wasn't sure how long she lingered. Eventually, she banged the chamber of the pipe against her boot to empty it and then went inside. A lone candle was lit on the table. After she barred the door, she carried it to her room before she blew it out.

She lay on her back still in her shirt and undershorts. She'd taken her socks and trousers off, but instead of donning a nightshirt, she'd simply collapsed on top of the covers. When she rested her palm on her stomach she was reminded of that night in the hotel, and how she'd had her hand on Charlotte as they slept. Wes wanted to be close to her again but wasn't quite sure how to make that happen.

Finally, sleep found her. She rolled onto her side and tugged the blanket along with her.

CHAPTER TWENTY-EIGHT

Charlotte took the rifle from Wes. It was heavier than she'd expected. Wes had promised to teach Charlotte how to shoot, but that had been weeks ago now, right after she first arrived. Finally, Charlotte convinced Wes to follow through with the lesson. It wasn't that Wes didn't want her to learn how to handle the gun, it just seemed that some other distraction always got in the way.

They walked to the end of the planted field, far enough away from the barn so as not to bother Dusty or Ned. Although Dusty occasionally raised her head up from eating grass to check their whereabouts as they walked away from the barn.

"Aim it at that tree over there." Wes stood behind her and pointed toward the creek.

"The skinny one?"

"No, that thick tree to the left."

"How bad do you think I'll be?" The large tree was a huge target. Charlotte thought there was no way she could miss it.

"Start with something easy, okay?" Wes stepped behind her and helped her adjust her stance. "Stand with your legs apart, and your right foot back a little. The rifle will kick and you want to brace your stance so it doesn't knock you down."

Charlotte attempted to hold the gun aloft until the tree was in the sight, but the long rifle was heavy, and her arms began to shake. After a few seconds, she lowered the rifle.

"It's so heavy."

"Maybe we need to find something for you to rest the barrel on." Wes motioned for her to follow.

Charlotte trailed behind Wes, carrying the heavy weapon. Finally, Wes found a low-hanging branch of a sapling and assisted Charlotte in propping the gun on it.

"Okay, now, there are two triggers." Wes was standing very close behind her, speaking softly in her ear. "Place the tree in the front sight there." She pointed to the tip of the barrel. "Line it up here." Wes touched a notch nearer the stock of the rifle.

"Okay, I think I have it lined up." Charlotte closed one eye and rested her cheek on the wooden stock of the gun. Wes touched her elbow lightly to indicate she should raise her arm a little.

"Set the first trigger…and then the hair trigger will fire when you're ready—"

The gun discharged loudly, and if Wes hadn't been standing so close behind her, Charlotte would most definitely have fallen backward.

"Sorry!" Charlotte knew that Wes was holding all of her weight.

"It's okay. That happens to everyone the first time." One of Wes's arms was around Charlotte's waist, and with the other she supported the rifle so that Charlotte didn't drop it.

"Can I try again?" She found the entire experience exhilarating.

Wes laughed.

"Go right ahead."

The second time, Wes stood so close that Charlotte could feel Wes's chest against her back. Wes's strong arms helped her brace the gun. This time when she fired the rifle she was prepared for the jolt.

"I think you just killed your first tree." Wes grinned as she stepped away from Charlotte.

Charlotte immediately missed the closeness as she handed the heavy rifle to Wes. She'd have asked for another lesson, but she knew ammunition wasn't cheap. At least now if the need presented itself, Charlotte could fire their only weapon.

She noticed Wes looking at her and instinctively covered the curve of her stomach with her hand, almost in a protective gesture.

"The baby is starting to show isn't it?"

Wes nodded.

"I didn't mean to make you uncomfortable."

"Oh, you didn't." Charlotte wanted to share the experience with Wes. She wanted Wes to feel a part of the whole thing, otherwise, this arrangement would never work. "I just saw you looking at me as if you noticed."

"It suits you."

"What?"

"Being pregnant." Wes seemed uncomfortable with the topic. She shoved her free hand in her pocket and looked at her boots.

"Thank you."

"Are you scared?" This time Wes looked at her with a serious expression.

"Maybe a little." If she was honest or really thought about it, she'd probably have been terrified.

"Have you ever seen a baby being born before?"

"No, have you?"

Wes nodded.

Wes could see the shadow of worry pass over Charlotte's face. In truth, she was worried too. They were alone with no doctor or midwife for miles. They turned and walked toward the cabin.

"One of my cousins had a baby." Wes remembered the event well. She'd only been eight at the time, but she recalled the difficulty of the delivery. She didn't share any of those details with Charlotte. There was no point worrying Charlotte in advance. She didn't want to scare Charlotte, or herself, for that matter.

"Perhaps I'll talk to Maddie about it now that the baby is showing." The breeze ruffled her hair and Charlotte swept her fingers through it to tame the wild strands away from her face. "She has two children already, so she already knows a lot more than I do."

"That's a good idea." Wes set the rifle inside when they reached the house. Then she turned to Charlotte. "Would you like to go for a walk?"

Farm work didn't allow for much downtime and with the day's work finished it seemed like a nice idea to spend time with Charlotte.

"Yes, I'd like that very much."

"There's a deer trail along the other side of the creek that makes for a nice walk."

Wes patted Dusty's neck as they passed the barn. Once they reached the creek she realized it might be more complicated for Charlotte to cross with her long dress.

"I could carry you," Wes said.

"I'll be fine. I can hold my skirt up...if you'll help me." Charlotte held her hand out to Wes. "The rocks are slippery."

"Sure." Wes took Charlotte's hand and guided her across a shallow point in the stream, coaching her to step from rock to rock.

They were almost at the other side when Charlotte lost her footing. Wes caught her but sacrificed her right boot to the stream in doing so.

"Sorry!" Charlotte wrapped her arm around Wes's neck to brace herself, while still doing her best not to drop her skirt into the water.

Now that she was already standing in the water Wes decided to carry Charlotte.

"This might be easier." She reached under Charlotte's knees and lifted her easily into her arms. Charlotte wrapped both arms around Wes's neck.

"You can't carry me!"

"I think I'm doing it anyway." Wes grinned.

Charlotte laughed.

She reached the far side of the stream and Wes gently set Charlotte down but couldn't quite let go completely. Her hands rested at Charlotte's waist, and they were standing very near. Charlotte was looking up at her with a curious expression. She felt her heart flutter and her insides knot. She drew Charlotte closer and Charlotte didn't seem to mind. Charlotte's hands rested lightly on her shoulders.

What was she doing?

"I...I'm sorry..." Wes released Charlotte and stepped away. She swallowed and tried to dislodge thoughts of kissing Charlotte from her mind. They had an arrangement, but that was all. She reminded herself that they had a partnership, but not a true marriage.

"Don't apologize." Charlotte moved nearer. "I like being close to you, Wes."

Wes nodded, but she wasn't sure exactly what Charlotte meant and didn't know how to ask without revealing much more than she wanted.

She offered her arm to Charlotte. Charlotte smiled as she slipped her arm through Wes's. They strolled leisurely along the path that ran north and south between the stream and a huge swath of open prairie to the west.

"I've only ever been on the other side of the creek…our side."

Wes took notice that Charlotte said *our*. The thought that Charlotte considered them a team made her feel good.

"I come this way to hunt sometimes." Wes looked out over the open landscape.

"The view is almost too big to take in, isn't it?" Charlotte paused. "I think I focus on the space near the cabin because if I think of how far we are away from…well, everyone…. It can feel overwhelming."

"You're not sorry you made the trip west, are you?" Wes worried that Charlotte might have regrets at some point.

"Oh no, nothing like that." Charlotte turned to look at her. "It's just…different. That's all."

"It is, for certain." Wes rarely thought of Tennessee the past few years. This new land truly seemed like home to her. She suspected that the closeness of the terrain in Tennessee would feel almost claustrophobic to her now.

After a while, as the sun dipped lower, they returned to the creek crossing.

This time, Charlotte allowed Wes to carry her without complaint.

Charlotte rested her cheek on Wes's shoulder and Wes tried her best to focus on keeping her footing rather than on the tempting scent of Charlotte's hair. The best part of the entire day for Wes was the few moments in which she was able to hold Charlotte in her arms. She took special note of it. She couldn't help wondering if Charlotte had any of the same feelings about her.

CHAPTER TWENTY-NINE

Almost a month had passed since Charlotte's visit with Maddie. She'd been wanting badly to share the news of her pregnancy with Maddie, and now she'd hardly have to say a word, because it would be obvious the moment Maddie saw her. Ben had passed Wes one day in the field and had invited them to Sunday dinner.

Charlotte held a cloth over the pie she held in her lap. She tried her best to stabilize the dish as the wagon rocked back and forth over the uneven trail. She glanced over at Wes on the seat beside her and smiled.

"What?" Wes gave her a sideways look.

"You look rather handsome with short hair." As promised, Charlotte had cut Wes's hair for her a few days earlier. She was quite proud of her handiwork.

"Thank you." Wes looked ahead rather than at Charlotte. She seemed embarrassed by the compliment.

"I didn't mean to make you feel self-conscious."

"I'm not." Wes shook her head. "I'm just minding the horses, that's all."

Charlotte didn't believe her. She still found Wes's bashfulness endearing. Charlotte had never considered herself to be someone with a lot of self-confidence, but compared to Wes she was. Not that Wes wasn't confident. It wasn't that. Because if something needed to be done around the farm Wes was very sure of herself. It was more about personal, intimate moments that seemed to ruffle Wes's calm exterior.

Maybe Charlotte simply had more experience around other women. She'd shared a rented room with Alice in St. Louis. They'd shared everything with each other. In the time that she'd lived with her they'd probably become more like sisters than actual sisters. Charlotte actually needed to write her friend a letter to let her know she was safe and where she'd ended up. She'd hugged Alice good-bye with a promise to write as soon she arrived in California. It seemed that trip farther west would never happen now. And Charlotte was actually okay with that. Where she was now, here with Wes, seemed like the place she was supposed to be—the place she was meant to be. But how could she know that for certain? She wondered silently to herself. The honest answer was that she could just feel it.

The Caufield farm began to take shape in the distance, and she returned her thoughts to the moment at hand. As they neared the edge of the plowed field, Joseph ran out to meet them. He waved hello and ran alongside the wagon all the way to the house.

As she'd predicted, the moment Wes helped her down from the wagon seat Maddie smiled at her broadly.

"I can see we have a lot to catch up on." Maddie put her arm around Charlotte's shoulders and ushered her inside. "Sweetie, you go help your brother with the horses." Maddie shooed Rachel away from her skirts. "Let the grownups talk for a minute."

Charlotte set the pie pan down near the sink. She slipped her bonnet off and waited for Maddie. Something smelled good.

"She's always under foot, afraid she'll miss something." Maddie shook her head, but it was clear she wasn't really bothered.

"Rachel adores you." Charlotte couldn't wait to know what that sort of love felt like.

"Charlotte, you are fairly glowing."

"Does it show?"

"You are showing just a little. I'll bet Ben didn't even notice." Maddie rolled her eyes. "Men."

Charlotte had to laugh. She could see Wes and Ben from the window as they unhitched the horses and let them graze near the barn. Joseph and Rachel were running through the grass, chasing something.

"I'll be honest. It took me by surprise." Charlotte rested both palms on her stomach. That was a true statement, but not in the way Maddie probably assumed.

"Well, I'm very happy for you and Wes." Maddie motioned to a chair near the table. "Please sit while I check on dinner." She lingered by the table long enough to peek under the cloth covering the pie. "This looks delicious."

"I'm not sure the crust turned out perfectly, but hopefully it'll taste good. It's wild strawberry and rhubarb." Charlotte had discovered a patch of strawberries between the lower plowed field and the stream. The berries were small but had a sweet taste.

"I pounded some venison and used it for a stew, but it's mostly potatoes with some wild onions."

"It smells delicious."

"I think it'll be the biscuits with butter and your pie that save dinner."

They both laughed.

Maddie stirred the large pot hanging over the fire and then lifted the lid on the Dutch oven sunk into the coals to check the biscuits. "This all just needs a bit more time." Maddie closed the cast iron lid with a light thunk. She wiped her hands on her apron and turned to Charlotte. "I have some things you might like."

Charlotte followed Maddie to a chest in the corner of the room where Maddie pulled out baby clothes. Dressing gowns and a tiny blanket.

"You should take these." Maddie held one of the gowns up to Charlotte.

"Oh, no, I couldn't."

"Please, I insist. You'll need them before I will at this point."

"Well, if you're certain." Charlotte held the tiny, soft clothing against her chest. It was hard to believe that she would have a child so small, or that anyone was ever as small as this clothing. But she knew it was true.

"I don't really know anything about having a baby." Charlotte was afraid that her lack of experience was evident.

"You'll be fine." Maddie touched her arm. "Every woman feels overwhelmed by the thought of motherhood, but you will know what to do when the time comes."

"Do you really think so?"

"I do. And I'll be here to help." Maddie embraced Charlotte.

"I'm so glad we met, Maddie." The friendly hug soothed her.

"Me too."

❖

Wes stood next to Ben inside the sod-sided barn. Joseph and Rachel were inside the stall near the calf. The children doted on it like a pet. It occurred to Wes that she needed to figure out a way to get a milk cow for their place. With the baby coming she was sure they'd want the milk for butter and cooking among other things. Plus, the bit of butter that Charlotte had brought home from Maddie had been such a treat that Charlotte had been asking ever since then if they could have their own cow.

"I'd like to get a cow for our place." Maybe Ben could help with that.

"I know of a fellow who brings livestock to sell in Hollister from time to time." Ben wasn't looking at Wes. He was watching his children. "I think he would barter for a dairy cow."

"Do you happen to know when he'll be in Hollister again?"

"I'll be sure and find out and let you know."

They sauntered back to the house as Joseph and Rachel ran ahead of them. Wes couldn't help thinking of how much her life was going to change once Charlotte had the baby.

Charlotte was going to have a baby.

Wes was going to be a parent.

Those were two very scary thoughts. For a fleeting moment she considered asking Ben what it was like to be a father, but then she chickened out. They'd never really talked about those sorts of things, and he didn't really even know that Charlotte was pregnant, although Wes was pretty sure that Maddie had noticed the minute she'd laid eyes on Charlotte.

Men and woman lived such separate lives in some ways. And as the man in this arrangement, Wes was expected to follow those strict lines of division, but her emotions were becoming harder and harder to rein in. Wes was changing and she knew it was because of her feelings for Charlotte. What was she going to do about that? She'd almost kissed Charlotte by the stream that day. Why hadn't she just done it?

Because crossing that line might ruin everything.

How could she ever know for sure unless she crossed it? Even thinking it was too scary.

Wes was grateful that Ben wasn't much of a talker so she was allowed to be quiet with her thoughts as they strolled toward the house.

The sky was streaked with orange all the way to the western horizon. A few thin clouds, flat on the bottom as if they rested on an invisible shelf, were lit from beneath with hues of orange and pink. Wes paused for a moment to look at the sky. She never tired of the scope of the Kansas sky. It likely wasn't possible that the sky was larger here than in Tennessee, but it sure seemed like it was.

Wes smiled at the sunset and then turned and followed Ben inside.

They had only presented themselves as a couple on a few occasions. First, on the trip to find the circuit preacher to get married and now they were here for dinner with the Caufields. Wes tried to relax, but she couldn't help being aware of everything she or Charlotte did. Charlotte seemed so much more at ease than Wes felt on the inside. Ben and Maddie seemed to accept them as they presented themselves, so she tried to coax herself into relaxing and enjoying the comradery.

Dinner was enjoyable. Joseph and Rachel were very well mannered and polite children. Wes took special note of this. She knew nothing about parenting a child, but she would soon have to learn. That's assuming everything went well and Charlotte wanted her to be equally involved. They hadn't really discussed how exactly things would be once the baby arrived.

She'd been staring at Charlotte without realizing it until Charlotte smiled at her. Wes redirected her attention to the dessert in front of her.

"The pie is really good." She thought it would be polite to give Charlotte a compliment.

"Thank you." Charlotte seemed pleased.

"Yes, it is." Maddie chimed in. "The crust is especially good." Everyone was quiet for a moment until Maddie spoke again.

"Ben plays the fiddle sometimes. Perhaps we could get him to play for us."

"Yes, that would be lovely." Charlotte's face lit up.

"Oh now, don't go getting their hopes up. I ain't that good." Ben shook his head.

"Hush now. You *are* good and you know it." Maddie touched his shoulder as she reached past him to clear the table. "Come on, Rachel, and help me clear the dishes."

"I can help too," Charlotte said and started to get up.

"No, no…you sit. You're our guests." Maddie wouldn't hear of it.

Their cabin wasn't much larger than Wes's, but it somehow felt cozier. Perhaps because there were more places to sit. In addition to the benches and chairs around the table, there were two other seats near the fire. One had a soft-looking sheepskin draped over it and the other had a cushion over the woven chair seat. Wes considered that perhaps her own dwelling was a bit sparse and began to brainstorm ways to improve it for Charlotte's sake.

While Maddie and Rachel cleared the table, Ben retrieved his fiddle and began tuning it. Even the exercise of tuning the instrument was enjoyable. It had been a long time since Wes had been around anyone who could play music. Her grandfather and uncle had played back in Tennessee. As a wee child there'd been many evening concerts from the front porch of her grandparents' cabin.

"If we shift the table over a bit we'll have more room to dance." Maddie grasped one edge of the table and indicated that Wes should help her.

"Dance?" Wes didn't know how to dance. Her plan had been to simply sit and enjoy the music. But at the mention of dancing Charlotte's eyes began to sparkle and Wes knew she was in trouble.

Ben began to play a lively tune and the children immediately started to hop about. Charlotte took Rachel's hands, and they swayed back and forth. Maddie danced with Joseph. He was very serious, and she seemed to be trying to show him how to dance with a partner. Whereas Rachel was just joyfully dancing in circles and sweeping Charlotte along with her.

"Whoa...I'm getting dizzy." Charlotte laughed and released Rachel's tiny hands. She swayed a little and immediately Wes was on her feet, by Charlotte's side.

"Do you want to sit down?" Wes held Charlotte's arms to stabilize her.

"No, dance with me." Charlotte moved closer, placing one hand on Wes's shoulder and the other in Wes's palm.

Ben continued to play a joyful melody. The children held onto Maddie in a larger circle and continued to move to the rhythm of the song.

"I don't really know how to dance." Wes spoke softly so that only Charlotte could hear.

"Just hold onto me and sway to the music." Charlotte smiled up at her. "It's easy."

Wes did her best to relax, but holding Charlotte in front of everyone made her feel a bit exposed. Surely everyone could see how being this close to Charlotte made her heart race and her cheeks red. After a few moments, she realized that no one was really watching them very closely. Ben was on his feet, playing for his family, focused on them. He tapped one foot as he transitioned to another tune.

"This is fun." Charlotte was watching Ben and Maddie.

"Yes, it is." Wes only had eyes for Charlotte.

Charlotte stepped away from her so that their hands were clasped at arm's length apart. She began to dance in a slow circle and tugged Wes along with her. Charlotte was smiling and laughing. She seemed so happy. Her mood was contagious. Time with Charlotte lightened Wes's heart.

❖

They remained until well after dark. Wes lit a lantern and hung it at the front of the wagon to light their path for the ride home, but outside the glow of that circle was utter darkness. At one point the horses spooked and Wes suspected there was a coyote or wolf nearby.

"It's okay now." Wes tried to calm Dusty and Ned.

"That was a very nice evening." Charlotte was looking up at the night sky. "There are so many stars." She shook her head. "Whoa, it makes me dizzy."

The horses picked up their pace and Wes tried to rein them in. She didn't want to miss the trail in the darkness, or worse, end up stuck somewhere.

"They seem nervous." Charlotte had only just noticed.

"I think they smelled an animal a ways back."

"What sort of animal?" Charlotte pivoted on the seat to look behind them, which was pointless because there was no moon. It was far too dark to see anything.

"I'm sure it's gone now." She didn't want Charlotte to worry.

Charlotte slipped her arm through Wes's and slid closer to her on the wagon's bench seat.

The prairie was black, the horizon a barely visible line where the black grasslands met the deep purple of the nighttime sky. It was hard to imagine what it would be like to be lost out here or be farther west where the territory was even less settled. It did sometimes, especially at night, feel as if the little cabin was at the far edge of the earth and beyond that might lie all sorts of unknown dangers. The thought that Charlotte had intended to travel west on her own still haunted Wes. Anything could have happened, and in truth, it almost did.

Wes pulled the wagon to a stop finally in front of the dark house. She hopped down and rounded the wagon to help Charlotte dismount. The whole place was eerily quiet, as if they were the only two people on the Earth. Wes rested her palms on Charlotte's hips after she helped her down. She relished the tiny instances of closeness and sometimes tried to make them last. She didn't immediately step away from Charlotte, who was unable to move away because the wagon was at her back. Still, Charlotte didn't seem bothered by their closeness. Her fingers rested lightly on Wes's arms and once again, Wes thought of kissing her. She closed her eyes and imagined what that sort of intimate contact might feel like. Even just thinking of it made her insides ache.

"Wes, are you alright?" Charlotte whispered.

Wes opened her eyes and looked at Charlotte. No, she wasn't alright, not in the way Charlotte meant anyway. And still she didn't step away, she moved closer, until her torso touched Charlotte's stomach. Charlotte gently squeezed Wes's arms. Was that a signal? They'd danced, they'd been close, they spent every day and night together in the same house, and yet, Wes wanted more.

She angled her face nearer to Charlotte's, pausing momentarily before making contact. Charlotte didn't turn away from her so she pressed on until their lips met. Wes had never kissed anyone before, except for the chaste kiss on their wedding day, but had been able to think of little else these past few weeks.

After the brief contact between them she pulled back and waited for what might come next. Charlotte didn't push her away or act in anyway as if she was upset. Instead, Charlotte held Wes's face in her hands, tipped her face upward, and kissed her. Charlotte parted her lips and teased Wes's lightly with the tip of her tongue. As the kiss deepened, Wes wrapped her arms around Charlotte and held her tightly. Charlotte's fingers were in her hair and at the back of her neck. Charlotte's kiss was driving her crazy. The ache she'd felt deep down inside had settled further down. Now that's she'd made this first contact, she wanted even more.

She finally broke the kiss, breathing hard, she buried her face in Charlotte's hair.

"Oh, Charlotte." She held on for fear that if she let go Charlotte would pull away or somehow disappear. A silly fear, she knew, but it felt as if her heart was outside her body, beating wildly, out of control.

"Wes, I've wanted to kiss you for so long."

Wes took a step back and studied Charlotte's face.

"You have?"

"Yes. I just didn't…well, I didn't know how to let you know." Charlotte closed the space between them again. She wrapped her arms around Wes's waist and rested her cheek on Wes's chest. "Ever since that night in the hotel I've wanted to be close to you again."

"Me too." Wes made slow circles on Charlotte's back with her fingers.

"Should we go inside?"

Wes hadn't wanted the moment to end. It didn't have to end, did it? She was reluctant to release Charlotte, but it was getting late and she was sure that Charlotte was probably tired. However, she had no idea how she'd ever sleep now. The kiss had electrified her nervous system so much so that she feared she'd never rest again.

"Why don't you see to the horses and I'll get ready for bed."

"Let me light a lantern for you first." Wes carefully climbed the steps to the darkened cabin and felt around for the lantern on the table. She returned and used a stalk of straw and the flame of the wagon's lantern to light the second lamp. She handed the lantern to Charlotte. "I won't be long."

Wes led Ned and Dusty toward the barn to unhitch the wagon. She looked back just as the light from the lantern receded with Charlotte into the house.

CHAPTER THIRTY

Charlotte carried the lamp to her bedroom and set it on the rustic dresser. She stood for a moment looking at the narrow bed. She felt very sure of one thing. She didn't want to sleep alone.

Quickly, before Wes returned from the barn, she hurried to Wes's room and attempted to drag the entire bed into her room, but it was too heavy to move by herself. The posts at each corner were substantial and heavier than she'd expected. Not to be completely thwarted, she instead dragged the straw mattress off the frame and placed it in front of the fireplace. She did the same with hers. She shook out blankets to cover the two mattresses side-by-side and then came the pillows.

She knelt down and stirred the coals to bring the fire back to life. She added kindling and a couple of thin sticks of wood. Charlotte had just finished when Wes stepped through the door. Charlotte stood near the cozy bed she'd prepared for them on the floor, hoping that she hadn't taken things too far. It was impossible to read Wes's expression.

"Is this okay?" She motioned toward the bed on the floor.

Wes nodded and turned to place the bar over the door. Then she crossed the room to where Charlotte stood. Wes gently placed her hand on Charlotte's shoulder and softly, tenderly let her hand drift down the curve of Charlotte's back.

"I don't want to sleep alone." Charlotte took a shuddering breath as Wes stroked her face with her fingers. "The bed was too heavy to move—"

Wes covered her mouth with a kiss. Charlotte gave in to Wes's insistent mouth, her luxurious mouth, and the sweet taste of her tongue as it teased Charlotte's. Wes dropped to her knees at Charlotte's feet. She helped Charlotte out of her shoes and then kicked her own boots off. She remained in a kneeling position looking up at Charlotte. She held Wes's upturned face in her hands and then slowly began to unfasten her dress. She slipped it off her shoulders so that the long skirt pooled at her knees. Wes held her hand as she stepped out of it and then she lay on the bed in her slip.

She reclined on her side and watched in the warm glow of the fire as Wes removed her vest, unbuttoned her shirt, and loosed her trousers. Wes had lately not been wearing the wrap beneath the undershirt and instead, was wearing a vest to further disguise her chest. Wes settled next to Charlotte in her undershirt and long briefs.

"Are you sleepy?" Wes's hand was on her arm.

"No, are you?" Charlotte scooted closer so that the curve of her stomach was against Wes's.

"I don't think I could sleep right now even if I wanted to."

They were quiet for a moment. They were both studying each other as if seeing one another for the first time.

"Why did it take you so long to kiss me?" Charlotte was curious.

"I don't know." Wes brought Charlotte's fingers to her lips and kissed them. "I suppose I was afraid that you wouldn't feel the same way that I did."

"It's scary to care for someone, isn't it?" She remembered the betrayal she'd felt from Nathaniel. A tiny voice inside her head cautioned her to be careful, but she couldn't stop herself. Had Wes not come to her rescue? Had Wes not cared for her more than Nathaniel while barely even knowing her?

She sensed that Wes had very little experience with romance or sex. Her own experience was extremely limited, and only with one person, but still she probably knew more than Wes. Charlotte didn't want to rush anything, but at the same time her body ached to be touched. Perhaps it was that her body was changing because of the pregnancy and that her desire was amplified. Whatever the cause, she wanted Wes to touch her down there, but worried it was too soon.

Charlotte unbuttoned the front of her slip so that the shoulders drooped, leaving the fullness of her breasts on display. Wes watched intently but made no move to touch her. Charlotte reached for Wes's hand. She held it against her mouth and kissed Wes's palm. Then she placed Wes's hand over her breast. Wes lay very still, as if she was unsure of what Charlotte wanted, but didn't remove her hand. Wes looked at Charlotte with a questioning expression.

"You can touch me." Charlotte placed her hand over Wes's. "I don't mind."

It seemed that Wes needed permission and once it was given her boldness grew. Wes slid her hand inside the garment and caressed Charlotte's breast. Charlotte arched against Wes's hand, feeling the friction of Wes's strong fingers over her taut nipple all the way to her sex. As she caressed Charlotte, Wes kissed her mouth and her neck and then returned to her mouth. Charlotte slipped her hands past the hem of Wes's undershirt and trailed her fingers across Wes's ribs and up her back. At some point in the frenzy of mutual discovery, Wes partially rolled on top of her. She felt the press of Wes's thigh between her legs and rocked against it.

What had they done to each other? Now that she'd known Wes in this way she would have to have her again and again. There existed between them now a passionate tenderness, almost like a second sight, an ability to see in the darkness of another's soul. Wes had carried a lantern into hers. The shadows had been chased away and Charlotte was no longer afraid.

❖

The fire had almost completely gone out, but Wes could still sense the warmth of the glowing embers on her face. She was spooned against Charlotte's nude body beneath the blankets facing the fireplace. It was the very latest part of the night and Charlotte's slow, even breaths told Wes that she was still asleep. Wes closed her eyes and took a deep breath, inhaling the sweet scent of Charlotte's hair and skin.

Her arm was draped across Charlotte's waist. Her palm rested lightly on the soft, warm curve of Charlotte's stomach. Her nipples were pressed against Charlotte's shoulder blades. The warmth of Charlotte's body against hers was making it hard to sleep.

She'd never been with anyone the way she was with Charlotte. And now that they'd done things, she wanted to do more. She wanted to touch Charlotte again. She wanted Charlotte to touch her. Her body hummed and the place between her legs throbbed, and Wes considered waking Charlotte. Perhaps Charlotte was only in a shallow sleep and could be easily teased to wake.

Wes tenderly brushed Charlotte's hair away so that she could kiss the indent where her elegant throat met her delicate shoulder. As she kissed along Charlotte's shoulder Charlotte began to stir. She smiled and rolled over in Wes's arms. Charlotte snuggled against Wes's shoulder.

"You're awake." Charlotte's statement was soft and full of sleep.

"I'm sorry I woke you," she whispered, even though she wasn't the least bit sorry and she was sure Charlotte knew it. Wes felt caught up in some fevered state, and if she was to wake in the morning and discover all of this was no more than a dream, then she wanted never to wake. Or at least she wanted to make the most of the dream.

She sensed Charlotte's smile against her chest as Charlotte's fingers traveled down across her stomach to the sensitive, throbbing place between her legs. Charlotte raised up just enough to kiss her as she explored with her fingers.

CHAPTER THIRTY-ONE

Charlotte didn't wake all at once. She drifted toward wakefulness like one traveled toward the inviting light at the end of a tunnel. She blinked, realizing that the cabin was bathed in light from the open door. She was alone under the blanket and felt the other side of the bed for warmth. Wes was gone. She sat up, holding the cover against her chest to cover her breasts and swept her fingers through her hair hoping to clear some of the cobwebs from her brain with the same motion.

"Good morning." Wes stepped through the door, backlit by the morning sun. "I thought you might be hungry, so I went in search of eggs."

Wes set three eggs on the table and then knelt by the hearth to stoke the fire. Charlotte couldn't quite tell if Wes was feeling as awkward as she was. It didn't help that Wes had managed to get dressed while Charlotte was still in a serious state of undress.

"You let me oversleep." Charlotte had slept better than she had in weeks.

Wes stopped what she was doing and rotated on her knees to face Charlotte.

"I wanted you to sleep." Wes kissed Charlotte affectionately on the cheek.

"Thank you." Maybe Wes didn't feel awkward after all. "I should get dressed."

Charlotte stood and carried the blanket with her as she got to her feet. She wrapped it around her body, scooped up her discarded clothing, and carried them to her room. She dressed behind the drawn quilt, even though she wasn't sure why. And then she made her way to the privy, stopping at the well to splash water on her face.

When she returned to the cabin, breakfast was well under way.

"Do you need help?"

"No, you just sit and relax." Wes glanced over her shoulder. "It's almost ready. I warmed the leftover biscuits from yesterday too."

As Charlotte waited, she realized how hungry she was—starved in fact. But otherwise, she felt good. She felt really good, better than she'd felt in days or maybe weeks.

She watched Wes serve scrambled eggs onto two plates and wondered if things would be different between them now. For an instant, a tendril of fear ran through her system. What if sex ruined everything? But Wes didn't seem upset or distant.

Wes sat across from her. It was impossible to tell what Wes was thinking. She couldn't even sort out her own thoughts lately, much less those of someone else. The notion that two women could be together in the way she'd been with Wes had never occurred to her before. But she found the whole experience incredibly satisfying. It made so much sense that it would be. Women knew how they liked to be touched—how and where to be touched.

If Charlotte hadn't met Wes would she have ever been so bold? Probably not. But she'd felt an attraction for Wes that had only grown stronger the more time they'd spent together. She wanted to know if Wes was feeling the same way.

"Are you okay this morning?" She paused. "With what we did last night?"

Wes nodded and swallowed. She took a sip of coffee.

"Are you okay with it?"

"I am." Charlotte reached across the table for Wes's hand. "I…I'm happy."

"Me too." Wes squeezed her fingers lightly and smiled.

They ate quietly for a few minutes.

"I was thinking that we could put the beds together if you like and then we'd have the spare room for the baby when it comes." Wes had obviously been giving this some thought.

"I would like that very much." It touched Charlotte that Wes was thinking ahead about the baby. She hadn't even gotten a chance to show Wes the baby clothes that Maddie had given her.

"Well, as soon as we finish eating we can move things around." Wes smiled over her coffee cup.

And just like that it seemed they were going to continue to share a bed.

Why not? After all, they were married to each other. Charlotte smiled.

❖

Wes left Charlotte sewing in the cabin later in the day. She was making a new flowered print dress. The fabric was pale green with pink and yellow flowers. Charlotte had purchased the cloth in Emporia after the wedding.

They'd moved the two narrow beds side by side to make a larger bed that they could share. Wes had lashed the posts together using thin strips of leather so that they wouldn't move apart. After setting everything in place Wes had announced she was going fishing and had offered for Charlotte to join her. But Charlotte wanted to finish her sewing project so that as the baby grew she'd have a more comfortable dress to wear.

There was a lightness in Wes's steps as she walked. The thought that Charlotte would be waiting for her when she returned added to the sun's warmth on her skin. The thought that at the end of the day they would sleep close again made her smile. The thought of sharing a bed with Charlotte made her want to hasten the day to bring the nighttime.

There was a deep spot in the stream a little south of the farm that was a perfect fishing hole. It rained a day earlier, and the stream was swollen, but not too high. The bank was higher as she approached the fishing hole. Two large granite boulders were sunk partially into the bank creating a cleft between the rocks. A cottonwood grew at the crest of the bank, and its roots reached down on either side of the huge stones in search of soil and water. The air near the water's edge was cool and smelled of moss and damp earth.

Wes dug nearby for worms, and after finding a few, set one upon her hook and looked for a comfortable spot to sit before dropping it into the water. It had been a while since Wes had taken time to fish. There were always too many tasks to be done around the farm, but today seemed like the day for a bit of time away with her thoughts.

She sat quietly with her back against the cool granite boulder and waited. Her head was swimming with notions of the future.

Wes had always pictured herself as apart, alone. This new reality with Charlotte was causing her to rethink the way she'd ordered the world in her head. She was no longer alone. She'd had her brother for company, but this was very different. She'd never experienced the sort of intimacy with anyone that she'd shared with Charlotte. The sensation of this new experience was simultaneously exhilarating and terrifying.

Charlotte was only in the early stages of the pregnancy and Wes wondered how things would change as that progressed. She and Charlotte hadn't talked about having a child around the place or what that might mean for Wes specifically.

Wes didn't want to overthink things and ruin the gleeful feeling she'd enjoyed all day. She shook her head to dislodge any doubts. There would always be time for doubts, the world was full of doubts. For now, she wanted to relish this moment of happiness and reside in it as long as possible.

She felt a tug at the line and refocused on the fishing pole, which was basically a long birch branch with a string tied at the end. Wes waited patiently for one more solid jolt of the line and then she stood and backed away, bringing the fish along with her until she was able to yank the thrashing creature up onto dry land. The bream was small, but if she caught one or two more, then they would make a nice meal. She ran a small stick through the lower lip to hold it and then baited the hook again.

CHAPTER THIRTY-TWO

It was late and Wes had already undressed and gotten in bed. Charlotte tried not to watch Wes undress from the other room, but it was hard not to notice details of Wes's body. From behind, her shoulders were broad and leanly muscled. The muscles over her ribs flexed as she removed her shirt. Her waist was slim and her hips narrow. It was easy to see how she was able to disguise her sex. It was only when Charlotte caught a brief glimpse of Wes's small breasts in the candlelight as she slipped on her nightshirt that there was any indication that Wes was a woman.

The space was small, so Charlotte waited for Wes to undress before she did the same. She undressed with her back to Wes and slipped into her nightgown. Wes lifted the blankets for Charlotte when she climbed into bed beside her.

Charlotte was feeling tired. As the baby grew, her back sometimes ached and she at times felt needy for no reason. She wanted to be held and cherished, so Wes's suggestion to sleep together soothed her. Hopefully, she'd sleep better with Wes beside her in bed.

Charlotte had also been feeling inspired to get things in order for the baby's arrival, so Wes's suggestion that they use the second room for a crib was appealing. The urge to nest was almost overwhelming. She wanted to spend the next few months creating a cozy home for her family.

She snuggled close to Wes, resting her palm in the center of Wes's chest. For a moment she remembered their intimacy from the previous night, and she longed to feel it again. She wasn't exactly sure how to initiate it.

"Can I ask you something?"

"Sure." Wes had one arm propped behind her head and was looking up at the ceiling.

The only light in the room was the indirect glow of the waning fire in the adjoining room, making it hard to read Wes's expression, so Charlotte pressed on.

"I noticed when you were changing that you have a scar here." Charlotte lightly touched Wes's side, just below her ribs.

"This?" Wes lifted her shirt so that the angry red scar was visible against her pale skin.

"Yes." Charlotte tenderly traced the scar with her fingertip.

"It was a knife fight in St. Louis." Wes sounded rather proud about it. "You know that hunting knife I carry?"

"Yes." It was hard not to notice the weapon that Wes always kept with her. The handle was carved from a deer or elk horn.

"I won it in that fight after the fellow tried to cut me with it."

"What was the fight about?"

"He said something to my brother, challenging his manhood, that I didn't appreciate."

"Really?"

"Yeah, Clyde was a sensitive, quiet guy, so he was an easy target sometimes."

This was a different side of Clyde that Charlotte hadn't heard about. She'd always assumed that Clyde was Wes's protector, but perhaps they protected each other. Charlotte kept her hand under Wes's shirt. The light contact with Wes's warm skin was causing her insides to churn.

"How is your scar?" Wes rolled partway onto her side and brushed Charlotte's hair away from the spot on her temple where the bullet had grazed her skin.

"Oh, I forget it's even there." That was the truth. She hardly thought about it, despite the fact that it was the reason she was here in the first place.

Charlotte couldn't help letting her fingers travel beneath Wes's nightshirt. Wes tipped Charlotte's face upward and kissed her, softly at first, but then as the kiss deepened, she felt Wes's hand at her lower back pressing her against Wes's firm torso.

The sensations of Wes's touch at the hem of her gown and then beneath it and then between her legs were like a warm tide washing over her. As Wes entered her, she allowed the tide of emotions to carry her out beyond fear, trusting that if she allowed herself to love Wes that Wes would love her back. She hoped that in the innocence of this new discovery they could sail through these first moments of sensual hunger to someplace solid that they could return to again and again.

Wes was partway on top of her now, bare-chested and trailing tender kisses along her neck. Charlotte felt the orgasm build until she crested the wave and crashed beyond it. She clung to Wes's shoulders, sinking her fingernails into Wes's back. Her heart pounded and flames spread beneath her skin, blacking out everything except the roar of rushing blood in her ears.

"Don't let go," she whispered desperately against Wes's shoulder.

"I won't let go." Wes's response was breathy as she arched against Charlotte.

Searching in the dark with urgent fingers, she found Wes's face and drew her down into a fierce kiss.

❖

The morning came softly.

Charlotte lay awake, folded in Wes's arms, as the first pink hues whispered through the open window and lit the bedroom wall. Wes's deep even breathing told her that Wes was still asleep. Wes's arm was draped over her stomach. She gently entwined her fingers with Wes's, inhaled deeply, and then exhaled slowly. She closed her eyes and savored this moment of quiet affection as she folded her body against Wes.

Soon there would be no quiet moments. Or at least, she was anticipating the baby's arrival and the end of sleepy, slow mornings. Charlotte was sure she wouldn't mind that either, but at the same time she was grateful for these weeks of time alone with Wes. Whatever relationship they forged now would serve them well as a couple parenting a newborn.

They hadn't really discussed the idea of parenting and sometimes she wondered if Wes had truly grasped the fact that she too was going to be a parent.

Charlotte sometimes sensed the baby's fluttering movements. It felt almost like butterfly wings. Her stomach was really beginning to show the baby's growth, but she hadn't felt it kick yet.

As the light in the room turned from pink to orange, she returned to thoughts of her coupling with Wes. She realized now that she'd suffered from a loneliness she'd hardly let herself call by name. She'd suffered hurts from others and losses of faith, and perhaps this had made her accept her separateness as inevitable and unavoidable. Wes was showing her a different path.

As Wes began to stir, she raised Wes's fingers to her lips and kissed them.

CHAPTER THIRTY-THREE

Maddie waved to Charlotte as she approached the cabin. Charlotte set the washing aside and waved back. She walked toward Maddie, and they embraced at the edge of the yard, then turned and walked back toward the house arm in arm.

Charlotte hadn't seen Maddie in a month and was very excited about the surprise visit.

"I hope I'm not intruding."

"Absolutely not. I'm so pleased to see you." Charlotte squeezed Maddie's shoulders. "You left the children with Ben?"

"I did." Maddie's expression was playful. "Honestly, I just needed a moment to myself. Soon you'll understand what I mean."

"I'm sure you're right." Charlotte smiled.

Wes smiled and waved from the field. Maddie waved back.

"I don't know if I've ever seen Wes smile like that." Maddie nudged Charlotte with her shoulder. "I think you've made Wes very happy."

"I am really happy too."

"I'm so pleased for you two." Maddie followed Charlotte into the cool interior of the cabin. "And for myself because now I have you as a friend." She removed her sun bonnet and tamed her hair with her fingers.

There was a tiny internal tug for Charlotte to tell Maddie the truth about her relationship with Wes. But how could she? Yet, how could Charlotte have a deeper friendship with Maddie if she wasn't truthful. What sort of friendship did they have if she didn't truly trust Maddie with the thing that meant most to her. She'd wrestled with these thoughts but hadn't decided how best to deal with them. And the truth was, it wasn't just her secret to share. By sharing the truth, she put Wes at risk too. That was a bit too scary.

"I'm so glad we met." Charlotte kissed Maddie lightly on the cheek. "Shall I make us some tea?"

"That would be great, thank you." Maddie set the basket she'd been carrying over her arm on the table and searched under the cloth covering. "I made us some tea cakes."

"Oh, wow." Charlotte leaned over to take a look at Maddie's reveal.

"They might taste more like biscuits, but at least they have sugar in them." Maddie grinned. "Honestly, I don't even really know what tea cakes are, but they sound fancy."

"Well, whatever we call those, they look delicious."

"How are you feeling?" Maddie sat at the table while Charlotte heated water.

"You can probably imagine…I feel like I weigh a thousand pounds." Charlotte rested her hands on her hips as she stood near the hearth. "I've been having leg cramps at night, but Wes has been rubbing my calves and feet, so that helps."

"Enjoy it while it lasts. Soon you'll both be too sleep-deprived to notice each other's needs." Maddie shook her head. "And if you have more than one, forget alone time."

Charlotte laughed.

"I'm sorry, I don't mean to laugh."

"No, you should laugh now, because soon you'll be too exhausted."

They both laughed.

After a few minutes the kettle was ready, and she poured hot water through loose leaves into the tea pot she'd brought with her from St. Louis. It was a dainty bit of china painted with small blue birds and one of the few items that gave a clue that a woman lived here. Wes didn't have any sort of dishware that wouldn't be equally useful while camping out in the wild.

"That's a sweet teapot." Maddie examined it more closely.

"It belonged to my mother." Charlotte sat down across from Maddie. "She passed away several years ago. I wish she could see me now."

"Would she be surprised?"

"I think she would. I also think she'd be proud of me for making this trip." Charlotte rubbed her finger over an imperfection in the wood surface of the table. "She always wanted to get away from the city and live on a farm, but never got the opportunity."

"Well then, I wish she could see you now too." Maddie reached over and covered Charlotte's hand with hers. "Who knows, maybe she can."

"Maybe she can." Charlotte smiled.

Charlotte used her apron to dab her eyes.

"I swear, I don't know what's wrong with me. I'm giddy one minute and nearly in tears the next…my emotions are all over the place." She looked up at Maddie. "And I'm suddenly so sentimental about…*everything*."

"It's called motherhood." Maddie's mouth quirked up in a half smile.

"Well, you're no help." Charlotte playfully swatted Maddie's hand and they both laughed.

"What's so funny?" Wes was standing in the doorway watching them.

"Maddie just told me I'm pregnant." Charlotte grinned. "Imagine that!"

❖

Maddie stayed for another hour before gathering her things to leave. They'd had a lovely afternoon. It warmed Charlotte's heart to have a friend. She decided to walk partway with Maddie along the trail. It was nice to walk and get a different sort of exercise that didn't involve bending over. Her back had a regular ache these days.

After a little while, Charlotte decided to turn back. It was getting late and she wanted to get home in time to make something for dinner. Wes had cooked the previous night to give her a break so she wanted to hold up her end of the arrangement. She was ever aware of how much she still needed to learn about farming and she didn't want Wes to be carrying more than her share of the workload. Charlotte needed to feel that she was contributing in a valuable way, for Wes's sake.

"Thank you again for the visit, Maddie." Charlotte took Maddie's hand. "Your friendship means a lot to me."

Maddie's expression grew serious.

"What's wrong?"

"Nothing's wrong." Maddie squeezed her fingers lightly. "You call on me when the time comes okay? I mean that."

Charlotte nodded. She thought she might even start crying again.

"You tell Wes to come get me and I'll be there in an instant. There's no need to be afraid. You're going to be an amazing mother."

Charlotte hugged Maddie. A good friend told you just what you needed to hear when you needed to hear it most.

"Thank you," she whispered.

❖

As she walked back and reached the edge of their farm, Charlotte stopped to gaze out at the fields. The crops had grown tall, the clear and literal fruit of their labors. How different her life had become. She thought back to her days working at the hotel. Now she was living her own adventure instead of always watching others embark on theirs. Thinking of her friend, Alice, in St. Louis, she decided she would finally sit down and write a letter. They could mail it from Hollister the next time they traveled there to pick up supplies.

Wes was tending to the horses when she neared the cabin.

"How was your visit with Maddie?" Wes had been moving hay around. She stopped and leaned against the long handle of the rake.

"It was a nice break." Maddie held her arms across her stomach. It had been nice to take a leisurely walk. "She offered to come when the baby is ready to deliver."

"That would be good." Wes looked relieved.

"I'm going to make some supper for us."

"Thank you." Wes smiled. "I've got a little more to do then I'll wash up and come in."

Charlotte turned toward the house. She'd been here long enough that this place was really beginning to feel like home. As she crossed the threshold, she remembered her first impression of the place and how she'd wondered if it was abandoned. As it turned out, the little house just needed some love and attention to turn it into a home.

She watched Wes from the kitchen window as she worked the biscuit dough with her hands. Her heart was as light as the warm summer breeze that came from the open door.

CHAPTER THIRTY-FOUR

Wes had been working for weeks on finishing the root cellar behind the barn. It was a project that she and Clyde had started but had fallen aside to make way for more urgent work. But since harvest was upon them Wes wanted to finish the small storage building to keep animals out of the dried meat and vegetables stored there. Constructed properly, it would also maintain a constant cool temp since it was nearer the creek and shaded by the back wall of the barn. They'd purposely set to digging so that that the back wall of the root cellar was as close as possible to the thick sod wall of the barn.

After weeks of work in the evenings, the cellar floor was sunk several feet below ground level. The walls of the narrow structure were constructed of a mixture of sod and timber. She'd used the same materials for the roof, laying rafters close together and then adding the mud and sod on top. The roof and walls would well insulate the interior from temperature and weather changes.

Wes had used an awl to chink out a hole in the door so that she could add a leather loop that would act as both handle and latch. The finishing touch. She stepped back to admire her work. She'd worried that she'd never finish it working alone, but she had. Nights when Charlotte spent time sewing or knitting things for the baby, she was outside working, sometimes past dark with only a lantern.

Charlotte was very pregnant at this point and needed a bit more time to rest in the evening. Wes certainly didn't want Charlotte to help with the heavy labor of digging out the cellar or hoisting the timber for the roof.

Wes had noticed that with Charlotte's good cooking and the additional labor, that her upper body strength had increased. She had more stamina and her arms were so much stronger. Wes felt that, thanks to Charlotte, she was becoming her best self. She stepped back and admired her handiwork.

❖

Charlotte could see the glow of the lantern coming from behind the barn. She knew that Wes had been working on the root cellar, but sometimes she couldn't help wondering if Wes had used the task to get away from her. Was she that fussy to be around? She tried her best not to complain, but the baby was making it hard for her to sleep. Perhaps this was nature's way of getting her used to a lack of sleep when the infant arrived.

Either way, she wanted to see what Wes was up to. She was tired of sitting and needed some fresh air.

"Are you ever coming inside?" She hadn't meant the question to sound so sharp, but her emotions sometimes got away from her.

"Yes." She could tell Wes thought she was mad.

"I'm sorry, I didn't mean that the way it sounded." She shook her head.

"It's alright." Wes wiped sweat from her face with her handkerchief and then shoved it into her back pocket.

"No, it's not. I'm not feeling well, but I shouldn't take it out on you." She paused and then couldn't stop the question she blurted out all in a rush. "Are you avoiding me?"

"What?" The question obviously caught Wes by surprise.

"You're out here every night lately…forever—"

"No, absolutely not." Wes put her arm around Charlotte. "I am not avoiding you."

"Are you sure?"

"Trust me. I'd much rather be with you than doing this, but look, it's finished." Wes held the lantern up so that she could see the door in place.

"It looks very solid. The walls are so thick."

"It's supposed to keep the cool in and the heat out." Wes turned to look at her with a playful expression. "Do you want to see one more thing?"

"Yes...maybe..." Based on Wes's expression, she wasn't quite sure.

Wes took her hand and led her to the barn. In the back of the last stall there was a lump of something covered with a burlap tarp. Ned and Dusty lifted their heads as they slipped past them. Dusty rotated so that she could eavesdrop on their conversation.

"Here, hold this for a minute." Wes handed her the lantern.

Now she was really curious.

"I've been working on this too. I wanted to surprise you." Wes grinned. She held the corners of the tarp but didn't immediately reveal what was underneath.

"What is it?" She leaned closer.

Wes gently lifted the covering away, and underneath was a cradle. Charlotte couldn't believe her eyes. The body of the cradle was made of woven strands of birch, like an intricate basket. The rockers were made of bent willow branches skinned of their bark. And in each end piece was carved the shape of a heart.

"Did you make this?" Charlotte ran her fingers along the soft weave inside of the bed area. The slats were sanded smooth as silk and the weave was airtight. Moses couldn't have had a better basket for his trip down river. This looked as if it would hold water, or keep it out if necessary.

"It's been a long time since I used my caning skills. I learned from my aunt how to repair cane-bottomed chairs and baskets."

"Oh, Wes, it's beautiful and perfect." Tears gathered at the edge of her lashes. She leaned against Wes and wrapped her free arm around Wes's waist.

"Don't cry." Wes wiped away a tear with her fingers.

"I feel so silly and stupid for worrying that you were trying to avoid me." She took a shuddering breath. "And here you were, making a cradle for the baby. I don't know what's wrong with me."

"Hey, it's okay." Wes hung the lantern on a nearby peg along one of the support posts and then drew Charlotte into a hug. "I'm not upset with you."

"You know we're in this together, right?" Even though the cradle seemed like an obvious sign that Wes was invested in the pregnancy Charlotte needed to say the words out loud. "I couldn't do this without you, Wes."

Wes could see that Charlotte was feeling emotionally fragile. Perhaps she needed to take more care to be sensitive. Wes kissed Charlotte's forehead and then rested her chin on top of Charlotte's head, holding her close.

"I'm here. Everything is going to be okay."

"Wes, you'll love the baby too, won't you?"

How could Charlotte even doubt that she would? This baby was part of Charlotte, who she cared deeply for. She held Charlotte at arm's length so that she could see her face.

"Charlotte, this baby will have nothing but love from me." Wes hadn't even told Charlotte she loved her, but she was fairly certain that she did. Perhaps she should say it now.

"I'm scared."

"What are you afraid of?" She held Charlotte close again. Maybe this was a time just to let Charlotte talk.

"I'm afraid something will go wrong, or that I won't know the right thing to do if something does truly go wrong."

"Shhh, you're just nervous." Wes rubbed Charlotte's back. "I'm here and, Maddie…nothing is going to go wrong."

Wes tried to muster all the confidence she could manage because she needed Charlotte to believe it too.

CHAPTER THIRTY-FIVE

Summer had faded into fall and the crisp scent of autumn was in the air. Dry corn stalks lay strewn in the field, the corn having been harvested and the plant debris left to mulch the earth for next season's planting. The harvest was over, the meat had been cured, the corn sold or ground into meal, onions and potatoes stored in the root cellar along with canned berry jam.

They'd done all that Wes could think of to prepare for the onset of winter and the baby's arrival. Charlotte was grateful for Wes and her focus on preparing them to survive the harsh months of snow and cold on the open prairie. Having never experienced a Kansas winter, Charlotte wasn't sure how tough it would be, but she could only imagine.

She'd spent weeks using any free moments to fill gaps in the log house with mud and straw in an attempt to keep the icy wind out of their home once the weather turned. Charlotte had worked on the task until late in the day. She shifted to indoor tasks. She was adding water to the large pot near the hearth when she heard Wes's voice.

"Hey, I have a surprise for you." Wes peeked through the open door.

"You scared me." Charlotte had been distracted and hadn't even heard Wes climb the steps. Wes had gone to Hollister for supplies earlier and she hadn't expected her back for another hour or so.

"I'm sorry." But she didn't seem sorry. Wes was grinning about something.

"What are you up to?" Charlotte set her meal preparations aside and followed Wes outside.

Standing, tied to a post was the most beautiful brown and white cow Charlotte had ever seen. The cow turned and looked at her with large, dark eyes as she absently chewed on dry grass from the yard.

"How did you—?"

"I bartered with a fellow in Hollister. I traded some of our corn and threw in a bit of money I had saved for emergencies."

"Wes, this is amazing." She threw her arms around Wes's neck and kissed her. She was as excited as a schoolgirl. But jumping about only made the baby kick. "Oh! I think the baby is as excited as I am." She took Wes's hand and placed it on her stomach. "Did you feel that?"

"I did." Wes's expression was full of awe and wonder.

"Wes, this is the nicest gift you could have given me."

"I wanted you and the baby to have milk and, well…a farm needs a cow." Wes rubbed the curly hair on the crown of the cow's head. "She's a beauty, isn't she?"

"Yes, she is." Charlotte touched the Cow's back and then petted her neck. The cow seemed very relaxed in her new home.

"Ever since you brought that fresh butter back from Maddie, I've been trying to figure out how to make this happen." Wes seemed truly proud.

"You are amazing."

Wes untied the rope harness from the post and led the cow toward the fenced enclosure near the barn. Charlotte trailed behind them.

"I saved all those dried corn stalks so we'd have plenty to feed her."

"I wondered what you were up to when you kept piling them near the barn."

Wes led the cow into the enclosure and then stepped out and closed the gate. Ned and Dusty were curious, but not curious enough to actually saunter over to greet their new neighbor.

"She needs a name." Charlotte rested her arms on the top fence rail. "What should we name her?"

"I think you should name her." Wes draped her arm around Charlotte's shoulders.

"Bluebell."

"Where did that come from?" asked Wes.

"I'm not sure. It just seems…right. We can call her Belle."

"I like it."

Wes walked to the wagon and lifted a wooden crate from the back.

"I'll take these into the house." As Wes passed, she could see a sack of flour and some canned goods that Wes had picked up at the mercantile in Hollister.

"Did you see Martha?" Charlotte remembered well her first encounter with the storekeeper's wife.

"Yes, and she asked me about a million questions." Wes shook her head. "You'll have to make the trip with me next time or I'll never hear the end of it."

Charlotte laughed. "I'd like that."

She lingered for a moment on the stoop after Wes disappeared into the cabin. She rested one hand on the doorframe as she scanned the view. The farm was truly taking shape. And now they even had a milk cow. Charlotte's heart swelled with thankfulness. Everything was going so well for them that it almost made her a little nervous. She took a deep breath and decided to simply enjoy the richness of her new life with Wes. She smiled to herself as she turned to follow Wes inside.

CHAPTER THIRTY-SIX

Charlotte straightened from the hearth where she'd knelt to lodge the covered cast iron skillet into the hot coals to bake their evening bread. She placed her hands on her hips and arched her back. Then swept her palm across her rounded stomach. The baby sometimes felt as if it was pushing against her lungs, making it hard to breathe. She found that these days she'd suffer from shortness of breath if she overexerted in the least.

Ooh. She braced against the table with one hand and pressed the other to her side. The baby was kicking more too. Knowing delivery could come at any time now, Charlotte had a heightened awareness of the slightest shift in the baby's position or activity.

Maddie had promised to come to assist when the time arrived. Just knowing Maddie would be there eased Charlotte's mind. Not that she didn't trust Wes, but neither of them had delivered a baby and, well, having someone on hand who'd experienced birth would be a big help.

Movement caught Charlotte's eye out the window. She walked to the open door to see if she recognized the rider. She'd hoped it was Ben, but as the man drew nearer, she could see that it wasn't Ben. He had the look of someone who'd been living out of saddlebags for a while. His beard was shaggy and his clothing dusty. The wide brim of his hat hid most of his other features but there was something oddly familiar about him.

Charlotte scanned the property for Wes.

She finally spotted Wes walking toward the house from the barn. Wes had seen the rider too. Charlotte stood in the doorway, and watched the rider mosey toward the house. Clouds had begun to gather, but rain hadn't yet arrived. A strange unsettling feeling washed over her. Charlotte felt the threatening, menacing presence of the man and he hadn't even spoken yet. She tried to signal her unease to Wes, but Wes was intently focused on the rider. This man gave her the same uneasy feeling she'd gotten from the men on the stage. She'd ignored her intuition that time. She wouldn't make that mistake again.

Wes watched the stranger approach. She glanced over at Charlotte willing her to recede into the safety of the cabin, but Charlotte stood frozen in the doorway. Wes wished for the rifle, but it was leaning in the corner near the hearth. She did have the hunting knife. She touched the horn handle once just to reassure herself. They'd been lucky. Rarely did they have any trouble here, but there was something about this fellow's manner that set her nerves on edge the minute she saw him.

He came to a stop, looked at Wes, and then at Charlotte, without speaking or announcing himself in any way.

"Can I help you with somethin'?" Wes stepped in front of Charlotte so the man would be forced to look at her.

"If I had this pretty thing for a wife, I'd treat her better than you do." His voice was dismissive of Wes and at the same time, condescending.

"What did you say?" Wes's heart thumped loudly in her ears and adrenaline surged in her system.

"I would buy her pretty dresses. I wouldn't make her work so hard."

"You best shut your mouth, mister."

"Or what?" He slowly wound his horse's reins around the horn of the saddle and casually dismounted.

Wes didn't respond. She was instantly worried for Charlotte's safety.

"You remember me, don't you, darlin'?" He was ignoring Wes and talking directly to Charlotte.

Wes glanced over at Charlotte. She had a stricken expression. "That day on the stage...we left you for dead." He took a step closer. "It took me a while to get here. But when I heard you had survived...well, I had to come back for you."

"You know this man?" Wes turned to Charlotte. She felt as if she were being cut out of her own life at the moment and it wasn't a good feeling.

"Not yet she don't."

"We don't want any trouble, mister. You should just be on your way." Charlotte sounded afraid.

This had to be one of the men who'd attacked the stage. How the hell did he find them?

"Who's going to cause a problem?" He sneered at Charlotte. "Your man, here?"

Wes didn't answer.

"You're not much more than a boy, are you?"

"Charlotte, get in the house and bar the door." Wes spoke to Charlotte without looking at her. "Do it now." She sensed movement behind her but didn't turn around. She hoped Charlotte would just do what she asked.

"I've come for the woman, and I'm not leaving without her." He took a step closer. "You might as well make your peace with the idea of it." He paused for a moment, then refocused on Charlotte. "What else you got in there? I've been on the trail awhile. I could use some grub."

He was clearly dismissing Wes. Was he simply trying to intimidate her by making her feel small in front of Charlotte?

Wes's heart rate increased to match the growing rage deep inside. She'd worked hard for what she had, so had Charlotte. She wasn't going to allow some drifter to show up and ruin everything. Not now, not after all she'd been through to get to where she was.

Fear knotted in her throat, and she tried to swallow around it.

She realized with absolute clarity that Charlotte and the baby were everything. Glancing over at Charlotte in the doorway, she could not remember her life before now. The things she enjoyed, her desires, nothing…literally nothing mattered but the baby and Charlotte. The fear of losing Charlotte gripped Wes like a vise.

Wes took another side step, placing herself again between the man and Charlotte.

"There's nothing of value in the cabin." Charlotte hugged herself. "And no food to offer. I'm sorry." Charlotte was obviously trying to diffuse the situation, but it wasn't working.

The man shifted his weight from one foot to the other, turned to the side, and spit. Then he glared at Wes.

"She needs a man and all she's got is you." He didn't go for his sidearm, but he kept his hand near it.

Sensing his next move, Wes stalled. She appealed to his higher self, assuming he had such a thing. It was hard to picture a civil person beneath the greasy beard and shabby, dust filled clothing.

"I'm unarmed."

"You've got a knife don't ya?"

"And you've got a gun."

He held his hands up in the air as if he were giving up, but she knew he wasn't.

"Just get on your horse and keep riding." Wes tried her best to sound firm. When she was really angry sometimes her voice cracked. Not this time.

"I don't think so, son."

Wes swallowed her fear. She wasn't about to let some stage robbing outlaw take her family away. She'd worked too hard and they'd come too far. He slowly sidestepped and she adjusted her position so that she remained between him and the cabin door. If he got past her and hurt Charlotte she'd never forgive herself. She honestly didn't care what happened to herself at this point, but by God, she wasn't going to allow anything to happen to Charlotte.

He was only a few feet away when he made a move to pull his gun and Wes launched at him, catching him by surprise. He fell backward with a thump, with Wes on top of him. He had the gun in his hand and she managed to interfere enough so that he dropped it. She rolled off him and grabbed for the weapon, but he grabbed her arm and tossed her aside as if she weighed nothing. The gun was close to her foot, so she kicked it. Then he kicked her.

When he made a second attempt, she grabbed his leg with one arm and sank her hunting knife into his boot. He howled and staggered backward, giving her time to get to her feet. Wes lost sight of the pistol in the dust they were stirring up. Her distraction allowed him to take a swing at her. She felt her head snap back from the force of his blow and she almost fell. She managed to duck his second swing and dove, shoulder first into his gut. But this time he didn't fall and instead drove his elbow into her back, causing her to drop to her knees.

He grabbed her by the collar and yanked her up. Somehow, he'd gotten the pistol despite Wes's best efforts, and he pressed it to her bruised ribs.

"Hold it right there." Charlotte was standing in the open cabin door with the rifle.

"Tell your woman to put that gun down or I'll blow a hole in you right now." He was pissed. The barrel of the gun dug painfully into her side. Wes could see the buck knife still sticking out of his boot but couldn't reach it.

The wind had picked up and dust and leaves swirled in the air between where they stood and where Charlotte stood, creating a surreal scene.

"I'm not afraid to use this." Charlotte tried to sound forceful, but Wes could hear the tremble in her voice. "I mean it. Let Wes go."

"Put the gun down or—"

Charlotte fired before he even finished his statement. The shot caught him in the shoulder and he reeled backward, dropping his sidearm. Wes fell to the other side, but recovered quickly and retrieved the revolver. He was on his knees, and from her seated position, Wes fired the pistol, hitting him in the thigh. He fell sideways. His arms twitched as he writhed in the dirt.

Wes staggered to her feet, reclaimed her knife, and assumed a defensive position. Once she was sure he wasn't going to get up, she ran to Charlotte.

"Are you hurt?" Charlotte dropped the rifle and reached for Wes, holding Wes's face in her hands. "I have no idea who he is, but he seemed so familiar. I never even saw their faces and then I blacked out. I could never forget that voice."

"I'm okay…and you're okay. We should get some rope and tie him up." Wes was out of breath.

"Wes, thank God you're not hurt."

Charlotte clung to Wes and Wes held her close.

"Here, keep the rifle on him while I fetch the rope from the barn."

Wes was sure that the sheriff they'd met briefly in Emporia would be more than happy to take this fellow off their hands.

"Oh!" Charlotte practically doubled over. She braced against the door frame.

Wes was at her side immediately. She couldn't help wondering if the unborn infant had sensed the danger or their fear.

"What's wrong?"

"It's okay. Just a cramp." Charlotte took Wes's hand and placed it on her stomach. Wes could feel the baby kicking. "The baby is just restless, that's all."

Wes looked over at the wounded drifter. He appeared to be unconscious. Blood pooled beneath his injured leg.

We got lucky. Wes hugged Charlotte for a long time, afraid to let her go.

CHAPTER THIRTY-SEVEN

Two weeks had passed since the drifter had shown up. Wes had gotten Ben to help her transfer the wounded man to Sheriff Billings. Luckily, they found the sheriff in Hollister so they hadn't had to travel as far as Emporia. Wes had been reluctant to leave Charlotte alone for too long. The time for the baby's coming seemed to be nearing. Charlotte was certainly uncomfortable and ready to deliver. It was becoming impossible to sleep or even sit comfortably, forget bending over to do chores.

They had been blessed. She'd thought it a hundred times since surviving the attack. There'd been no sign of any other trouble. Perhaps she could finally put that awful event on the stagecoach behind her. Charlotte sometimes still couldn't believe how close she'd come on two occasions to losing her life.

Wes had saved her in every way possible. And she had even managed to save Wes. They'd become a team of partners and it felt good.

It was afternoon when Charlotte returned to the cabin to prepare dinner when she felt the first intense pain. It passed fairly quickly so she dismissed it as a combination of fatigue and the baby moving inside, but then it happened again. Charlotte blinked and took a breath. She pressed her palm to the side of her stomach. Was she imagining it, or did the baby's position seem lower?

Ohh. There it was again. She braced against the table and searched through the window for Wes. Was it time? Was this what it felt like when the time of delivery arrived?

Charlotte went to the door, and as she took the last step from the stoop her water broke. She felt dampness on her thighs. This was too soon, wasn't it? She'd expected at least another week or two. But obviously the baby had other ideas. Or perhaps the stress of everything that had happened brought the delivery time on sooner.

"Wes!" She put her hand on the wall of the cabin and searched again for Wes.

There was no response, so she called out again.

"Wes!"

After a few minutes, she saw Wes jogging in her direction.

"What's wrong? Is something wrong?"

"I think the baby is coming." Charlotte grimaced and bent over from another contraction. "Oh, it hurts."

"What do you need me to do?" Wes assisted Charlotte back inside.

"Go get Maddie. Will you go get her now?"

"I'm on my way." Wes helped Charlotte to the bedroom.

"I'm not ready to lie down yet. There's too much to do." She needed to put water on to boil. Could she even manage that in her current condition? "Please fill the pot with water before you leave."

"Right." Wes grabbed the pot from the hook over the fire and dashed out to the well.

She was back quickly and set the pot over the fire to heat.

"I'll be right back." Wes kissed her cheek. "Don't worry."

Easy for her to say, thought Charlotte.

"Go! Go!" She waved her hand at Wes.

Wes saddled Dusty in record time and headed off at a fast clip toward the Caufield homestead. She was torn between doing what Charlotte asked and being afraid to leave her side at this critical moment. But if she remembered anything about childbirth it was that the delivery could take several hours, so she reminded herself that they had plenty of time.

She rode hard to the farm, pulling Dusty to a stop in a cloud of dust in front of the house. Maddie immediately appeared in the doorway, wiping her hands on her apron.

"Wes, what's wrong?"

"The baby is coming." Wes was out of breath from their sprint across the prairie trail. "Charlotte asked me to fetch you. Can you come?"

"Of course. Just give me a minute to let Ben know." She started walking toward the barn and Ben met her halfway. Wes watched them talk and saw Ben nod, then he waved his hand at Wes.

"Can I just ride with you?" Maddie took a coat from inside the house and slipped it on. The temperature had cooled, but the adrenaline in Wes's system hadn't even allowed her to notice.

She nodded to Maddie and extended her hand. Wes let Maddie use her boot as a step to climb up behind her on the saddle.

"Mommy, where are you going?" Rachel suddenly appeared.

"Charlotte is having the baby. You be a good girl and mind your father." She wrapped her arms around Wes's waist and they were off again.

Wes kept a slower pace this time out of respect for her passenger, but she was incredibly anxious to be home with Charlotte.

The sun was setting as they neared the cabin. The last orange threads of the day streaked across the sky toward the western horizon.

Wes offered Maddie her arm and used her body as a counterweight as Maddie slipped from the saddle. Wes dismounted and followed Maddie into the house. Charlotte was on the bed and raised up the moment she saw them. She looked relieved. The minute she saw Maddie, she slumped back on the bed.

"You go tend to the horse." Maddie paused before drawing the drape to separate the rooms. "We'll let you know when we need something."

Wes stood for a moment staring at the cloth strung from wall to wall, hiding Charlotte from view. She felt helpless. She hadn't really considered what would happen when Maddie arrived, but getting shut out hadn't even occurred to her. It should have, though. Maddie thought Wes was a man and this, what was happening now, this was women's work.

❖

Initially, the pains were ten to twenty minutes apart and lasted for about thirty seconds. Charlotte had been trying to pay attention to how often they came and how long they lasted. Now, the contractions were very close together without a break in between.

But the scariness melted away the minute Maddie arrived.

"I'm here, Charlotte." Maddie threw her coat over a nearby chair and took Charlotte's hand. "How far apart are they?"

Charlotte shook her head.

"Close…they're very close."

Maddie propped pillows behind Charlotte and shifted the blankets beneath her. Charlotte had managed to get out of her shoes and bloomers, but she was still wearing her dress.

"Can you stand up? We should take this off."

Charlotte nodded. She felt like she weighed a thousand pounds and that if she stood the baby might drop right out of her, but with Maddie's help she stood, and Maddie quickly undressed her. Charlotte settled back on the bed with only her cotton slip. It was damp across her chest from sweat.

"I'll be right back."

Charlotte watched Maddie leave and then return with a basin of hot water. Wes appeared at the edge of the drape for a minute holding some towels and scissors.

"Is everything okay?" She could hear the worry in Wes's question and felt sorry that Wes wasn't in the room.

But then a contraction set in and all she could think about was the pain. And even the pain ceased to matter, it was just everywhere.

"She's fine." Maddie took the supplies from Wes then pushed her out of the room. She returned to Charlotte and smiled as if she could read Charlotte's mind. "He'll be fine too."

"Ahhh!" Charlotte couldn't help crying out.

"It's okay, the baby will come soon." Maddie looked under her slip and nodded.

❖

Wes paced back and forth in the main room of the cabin. It was terrible to hear Charlotte's cries and not be able to go to her, but Maddie had insisted she stay out of the room. Wes swept her fingers nervously through her hair.

Every now and then the room would become silent. Wes would stop her march and stare at the curtain. But then the cries would start again and she knew that Charlotte was still in the throes of labor.

At one point, after a few hours, Wes attempted to sit on the stoop and smoke her pipe, but she was completely unable to relax. And shortly after that, Maddie called for her to bring more water and another blanket.

Wes knew that sometimes there were complications. She couldn't bear the thought of losing Charlotte to childbirth. They'd only just found each other. And after all they'd been through it didn't seem fair that she should suffer this risk because of a man who'd abandoned her. Her gut was in knots as she began to march again from one side of the room to the other. She figured she'd walked thirty miles, ten feet at a time.

Charlotte's cries gave way to a deafening silence. Wes stopped in the center of the room and waited, unsure of what the silence meant.

❖

"It's coming now." Maddie positioned herself between Charlotte's legs.

All decorum was gone. Maddie had seen Charlotte at her worst now. She knew the moment the baby crowned as it felt like the ring of fire between her legs would engulf her.

"Don't push, just breathe through it." Maddie coached her.

Charlotte was too exhausted to do anything but what Maddie told her. She was drenched in sweat, her hair plastered to her forehead. She was so tired. And then all of a sudden, she felt a big, warm gush. The next thing she knew, there was a squirming wet thing in her lap. When she heard the baby's first sounds she began to cry, floating on a cloud of euphoria.

Maddie took the infant briefly and returned the swaddled child to Charlotte's arms. Then she drew the curtain aside and smiled at Wes.

Charlotte looked up with wet tears on her cheeks. Wes looked stricken, as if she'd also been in labor.

"I'll let you two have a minute to yourselves."

Wes nodded, an expression of awe on her face, as Maddie stepped past her to go outside.

"Come and meet our daughter."

"It's a girl?" Wes seemed timid as she approached, as if she moved too quickly or spoke too loudly she'd spook them.

"Yes, we have a daughter." Charlotte held her hand out to Wes.

"I was so scared of losing you." Wes pressed her lips to Charlotte's forehead and then sank to the edge of the bed and really looked at the baby for the first time.

"You're not going to lose me, Wes. I'm okay. Everything is okay."

"Her fingers are so tiny." Wes touched the baby's hand with her fingertip.

"Do you want to hold her?"

"Are you sure?"

"Yes, here." Charlotte gently moved the baby to Wes's arms.

"She's beautiful." Wes seemed completely smitten.

"She is perfect." Charlotte leaned against Wes's shoulder and fussed with the blanket around the baby.

"We don't have a name." Wes couldn't believe they hadn't already settled on a name. But she thought they'd have more time.

"I have the perfect name for our baby girl."

"You do?"

"I want to name her Promise."

Wes was quiet for a moment as she held the newborn. And then she smiled.

"Welcome to the world, Promise."

CHAPTER THIRTY-EIGHT

A week had passed since the birth. Charlotte and the baby were doing well. Maddie had come by once to check on everyone. Charlotte felt bonded to Maddie for life. She would never forget all that Maddie had done for her.

The November air was chilly and the sky was a cool blue-gray. The grass was brown and the cleared field had lost its color. Charlotte wrapped a blanket around her shoulders and the infant in her arms and walked out to where Wes was standing by the fence near the barn looking at the horizon.

Charlotte had grown more accustomed to the stark beauty and isolation of the grassland vista. A landscape that was pure, free from stain or experience. She loved it. Although she was still well aware that it would be a lonesome place without Wes.

Being with Wes and now having the baby, Charlotte had experienced a sense of belonging and happiness that she never dreamed possible.

"Hi." Wes kissed the baby gently and then wrapped her arm around Charlotte's shoulders.

As Charlotte held Promise in the shelter of Wes's arm, she realized how truly happy she was. Whatever brought her to this place—fate, destiny, a higher power—with Promise in her arms and Wes by her side, the idea of forever, something she'd never really believed in, seemed within reach.

She turned to Wes.

"Do you believe in forever?" She'd never asked before.

Wes was thoughtful. She stared out at the open landscape for a moment and then turned to Charlotte.

"To be honest, I never thought much about it. But now with you and Promise, I want to believe in forever because that's how long I'll be in love with you."

Charlotte leaned into Wes.

"I love you, Wesley Holden." She met Wes's intense gaze. "With all that I am and all that I will ever be."

"I love you, Charlotte." Wes kissed her tenderly.

The baby began to fuss in her arms, and she broke the kiss with a smile.

"And you, little one, are forever's Promise."

The moment she uttered the words Charlotte knew they were true. The sort of abiding truth that only comes from finding love. Charlotte kissed her daughter and then rested her cheek on Wes's shoulder. The sun was high and bright, and the sky was as big as Charlotte's love for her little family who had carved out a life full of hope and wonder on the prairie frontier.

THE END

About the Author

Missouri Vaun spent a large part of her childhood in southern Mississippi, before attending high school in North Carolina and college in Tennessee. Strong connections to her roots in the rural South have been a grounding force throughout her life. Vaun spent twelve years finding her voice working as a journalist in places as disparate as Chicago, Atlanta, and Jackson, Mississippi, all along filing away characters and their stories. Her novels are heartfelt, earthy, and speak of loyalty and our responsibility to others. She and her wife currently live in northern California.

Books Available from Bold Strokes Books

A Second Chance at Life by Genevieve McCluer. Vampires Dinah and Rachel reconnect, but a string of vampire killings begin and evidence seems to be pointing at Dinah. They must prove her innocence while finding out if the two of them are still compatible after all these years. (978-1-63679-459-4)

Digging for Heaven by Jenna Jarvis. Litz lives for dragons. Kella lives to kill them. The last thing they expect is to find each other attractive. (978-1-63679-453-2)

Forever's Promise by Missouri Vaun. Wesley Holden migrated west disguised as a man for the hope of a better life and with no designs to take a wife, but Charlotte Rose has other ideas. (978-1-63679-221-7)

Here For You by D. Jackson Leigh. A horse trainer must make a difficult business decision that could save her father's ranch from foreclosure but destroy her chance to win the heart of a feisty barrel racer vying for a spot in the National Rodeo Finals. (978-1-63679-299-6)

I Do, I Don't by Joy Argento. Creator of the romance algorithm, Nicole Hart doesn't expect to be starring in her own reality TV dating show, and falling for the show's executive producer Annie Jackson could ruin everything. (978-1-63679-420-4)

It's All in the Details by Dena Blake. Makeup artist Lane Donnelly and wedding planner Helen Trent can't stand each other, but they must set aside their differences to ensure Darcy gets the wedding of her dreams, and make a few of their own dreams come true. (978-1-63679-430-3)

Marigold by Melissa Brayden. Marigold Lavender vows to take down Alexis Wakefield, the harsh food critic who blasts her younger sister's restaurant. If only she wasn't as sexy as she is mean. (978-1-63679-436-5)

The Town that Built Us by Jesse J. Thoma. When her father dies, Grace Cook returns to her hometown and tries to avoid Bonnie Whitlock, the woman who pulverized her heart, only to discover her father's estate has been left to them jointly. (978-1-63679-439-6)

A Degree to Die For by Karis Walsh. A murder at the University of Washington's Classics Department brings Professor Antigone Weston and Sergeant Adriana Kent together—first as opposing forces, and then allies as they fight together to protect their campus from a killer. (978-1-63679-365-8)

A Talent Within by Suzanne Lenoir. Evelyne, born into nobility, and Annika, a peasant girl with a deadly secret, struggle to change their destinies in Valmora, a medieval world controlled by religion, magic, and men. (978-1-63679-423-5)

Finders Keepers by Radclyffe. Roman Ashcroft's past, it seems, is not so easily forgotten when fate brings her and Tally Dewilde together—along with an attraction neither welcomes. (978-1-63679-428-0)

Homeland by Kristin Keppler and Allisa Bahney. Dani and Kate have finally found themselves on the same side of the war, but a new threat from the inside jeopardizes the future of the wasteland. (978-1-63679-405-1)

Just One Dance by Jenny Frame. Will Taylor Spark and her new business to make dating special—the Regency Romance Club—bring sparkle back to Jaq Bailey's lonely world? (978-1-63679-457-0)

On My Way There by Jaycie Morrison. As Max traverses the open road, her journey of impossible love, loss, and courage mirrors her voyage of self-discovery leading to the ultimate question: If she can't have the woman of her dreams, will the woman of real life be enough? (978-1-63679-392-4)

Transitioning Home by Heather K O'Malley. An injured soldier realizes they need to transition to really heal. (978-1-63679-424-2)

Truly Enough by JJ Hale. Chasing the spark of creativity may ignite a burning romance or send a friendship up in flames. (978-1-63679-442-6)

Vintage and Vogue by Kelly and Tana Fireside. When tech whiz Sena Abrigo marches into small-town Owen Station, she turns librarian Hazel Butler's life upside down in the most wonderful of ways, setting off an explosive series of events, threatening their chance at love...and their very lives. (978-1-63679-448-8)

Broken Fences by Jo Hemmingwood. Former army sergeant Seneca Twist has difficulty adjusting to civilian life until she meets psychologist Robyn Mason and has a place to call home. (978-1-63679-414-3)

Never Kiss a Cowgirl by Ali Vali. Asher Evans dreams of winning the National Finals Rodeo in Vegas, and Reagan Wilson wants no part of something that brings back the memory of what killed her father. (978-1-63679-106-7)

Pantheon Girls by Jean Copeland. Cassie Burke never anticipated the detour life was about to take when a meeting with a prospective client reunites her with a past love and reignites the star-crossed passion they shared twenty years earlier. (978-1-63679-337-5)

Roux for Two by Aurora Rey. For TV chef Chelsea Boudreaux and hometown boy Bryce Cormier, love proves as tricky as making a good pot of gumbo. (978-1-63679-376-4)

Starting Over by Nance Sparks. Jennifer has no idea if she can mend Sam's broken soul after the sudden loss of her wife, but it's never too late for starting over. (978-1-63679-409-9)

The Accidental Bride by Jane Walsh. Spinsters Miss Grace Linfield and Miss Thea Martin travel to Gretna Green to prevent a wedding, only to discover a scandalous passion—for each other. (978-1-63679-345-0)

Three Wishes by Anne Shade. A magic lamp, a beautiful Jinni, and a cursed princess make for one unbelievable story. (978-1-63679-349-8)

Undiscovered Treasures by MJ Williamz. For Cyl and her friends Luna and Martinique, life's best treasures often appear when you're not looking. (978-1-63679-449-5)

Curse of the Gorgon by Tanai Walker. Cass will do anything to ensure Elle's safety, but is she willing to embrace the curse of the Gorgon? (978-1-63679-395-5)

Dance with Me by Georgia Beers. Scottie Templeton mixes it up on and off the dance floor with sexy salsa instructor Marisa Reyes. But can Scottie get past Marisa's connection to her ex? (978-1-63679-359-7)

Gin and Bear It by Joy Argento. Opposites really can attract, and as Kelly and Logan work together to create a loving home for rescue cat Bear, they just might find one for themselves as well. (978-1-63679-351-1)

Harvest Dreams by Jacqueline Fein-Zachary. Planting the vineyard of their dreams, Kate Bauer and Sydney Barrett must resist their attraction while battling nature and their families, who oppose both the venture and their relationship. (978-1-63679-380-1)

The No Kiss Contract by Nan Campbell. Workaholic Davy believes she can get the top spot at her firm if the senior partners think she's settling down and about to start a family, but she needs the delightful yet dubious Anna to help by pretending to be her fiancée. (978-1-63679-372-6)

Outside the Lines by Melissa Sky. If you had the chance to live forever, would you take it? Amara Rodriguez did, and it sets her on a journey to find her missing mother and unravel the mystery of her own heart. (978-1-63679-403-7)

The Value of Sylver and Gold by Michelle Larkin. When word gets out that former Boston homicide detective Reid Sylver can talk to the dead, the FBI solicits her help on a serial murder case, prompting Reid to assemble forces once again with Detective London Gold. (978-1-63679-093-0)

When It Feels Right by Tagan Shepard. Freshly out of the closet Marlene hasn't been lucky in love, but when it comes to her quirky new roommate Abby, everything just feels right. (978-1-63679-367-2)